A girl could dream.

And this girl maybe did dream. About an angry man in boxers. Oh, Lord, those boxers.

She shook her head. No. No no no no no. She was on a Fresh Path to Independence, not a Do-dumb-stuff-with-your-landlord-even-if-it-looks-super-fun Path. And taming that angry bear who lived next door would definitely be trouble. She didn't want trouble. She didn't want to reform a bad boy. That stuff was not for her. If the bad boy wanted to change, he would change. A person can only be who he is. That's how she'd ended up getting anxiety hives when her last boyfriend talked about marriage. She was not a homebody. She was not a stay-local kind of gal, and she had been living her whole life as if she were.

She had enough trouble trying to figure her own stuff out; she didn't need to try to figure out someone else's.

No matter how tempting it was.

No amount of head-shaking could convince her that she did not want to see what those flexing muscles looked like up close. Fortunately, he was clearly a jerk.

But what a hot jerk.

Also by Sarah Title

Kentucky Home
Kentucky Christmas
Home Sweet Home
Snowed In

TWO
FAMILY
HOME

Love isn't complex…it's a duplex.

A Southern Comfort Romance

SARAH TITLE

LYRICAL PRESS
Kensington Publishing Corp.
www.kensingtonbooks.com

LYRICAL PRESS BOOKS are published by

Kensington Publishing Corp.
119 West 40th Street
New York, NY 10018

All Kensington titles, imprints, and distributed lines are available at special quantity discounts for bulk purchases for sales promotion, premiums, fund-raising, educational, or institutional use.

Special book excerpts or customized printings can also be created to fit specific needs. For details, write or phone the office of the Kensington Sales Manager: Kensington Publishing Corp., 119 West 40th Street, New York, NY 10018. Attn. Sales Department. Phone: 1-800-221-2647.

Lyrical and the L logo are trademarks of Kensington Publishing Corp.

First Electronic Edition: August 2015
eISBN-13: 978-1-60183-454-6
eISBN-10: 1-60183-454-3

First Print Edition: August 2015
ISBN-13: 978-1-60183-455-3
ISBN-10: 1-60183-455-1

Printed in the United States of America

For Shar,
For your friendship, support, conference partnering-in-crime, and your name. Next, I shall ask for a piece of your soul, but you're so generous I think you won't even flinch.

ACKNOWLEDGMENTS

Firstly, I must thank Dana Smook, (a) for having the best dog ever in Bruno Copperpot (RIP) and (b) for giving me the idea for this book, even though I think you were maybe just joking. That'll show you! I also received some art-world expertise from Kelly S. Williams, and if I got anything about the art world wrong, please punish me by buying one of her paintings. Because it ain't her fault. Her dog is also quite groovy (Hey, Miss Rizz!). Tallulah Tinklepants gave me some much-needed guidance on the inner workings of a small nursing home, which was very helpful because I was going to have, like, one nurse do the whole thing. The Jell-O was all my own doing. (And guess what, she has a really cute dog, too!) Also to Pam May (who does not have a dog . . . yet) for making the connection, and for helping me figure out plot stuff as we whiled away an idyllic summer afternoon on a pool noodle in the Elk River.

I also want to thank my editor, Alicia Condon, for having such faith in my work and for seeing the potential in the half-written gobbledy-gook I gave her in New Orleans. To be fair, the half that was written was utterly charming. Also, a big thank you to Louise Fury and the growing Team Fury at the Bent Agency. We are mighty, and we will take over the world.

Finally, thank you to Brock Savage for the Skype sessions that helped me solidify my plot (ugh, I hate plots), for the tag line, and for finding my dog as charming as I do.

Love isn't complex . . . it's a duplex.

Prologue

His nose was driving him crazy. There was something in the bushes around the big white house that he needed to get at. But no matter where he sniffed or dug or marked (the marking was really just for the heck of it), he couldn't get to that *thing*. His nose led him to the back yard. He had to pause a minute to find the loose part of the fence—okay, the part of the fence he might have broken in his enthusiasm to get into the yard. But this was no time to stop and feel guilty. He was afraid he would lose the trail of whatever it was he was tracking.

He followed his daily route. Start at the loose (okay, broken) part of the fence, then secure the perimeter by smelling every corner and making sure to mark anything that smelled like a bunny or a cat or any of the other furry creatures he sometimes saw back here. When that was done, he could venture farther into the open. Sometimes he would find something delicious to snack on—even though sometimes that didn't make him feel so good—but today he was determined to stay focused. The scent seemed stronger than ever—but what was it? Where was it? It had to be nearby . . .

The back door opened and the big guy stomped into the yard. That was the end of searching for now. The big guy would always stand in the yard for a while and look around. Sometimes he thought the big guy was looking for him. But he was really good at hiding and eventually the big guy would go into the garage. He'd make a lot of noise in there, then come out when it was dark. Plenty of time.

Whatever he was tracking, it was close. He was gonna find it.

Chapter 1

"It looks . . . nice."

Lindsey tried her best not to roll her eyes. She was twenty-six after all. Surely eye-rolling at her mom's not-so-subtle snobbery was something she should have left behind in Phoenix with her prom dress and her John Mayer poster.

It was affectionate eye-rolling, she told herself. And it was less out of annoyance, and more for the benefit of Mary Beth Brakefield, surely the most patient realtor in the country. They were only looking for a rental.

And this was the third apartment Mary Beth had patiently dragged Lindsey and her parents to. From the outside, Lindsey thought it looked like the best. Only a few stairs up to the front porch, unlike the last one that had three narrow flights up to the admittedly gorgeous top-floor apartment of a building that reminded Lindsey of an old-timey brothel. Plus, this one had a porch, and the porch faced some very cute storefronts across the street, and rolling hills beyond that. A wonderful place for morning coffee. The house was a duplex on a quiet street, which was a marked improvement over the old-and-not-that-charming apartments near the campus of Pembroke College.

The front yard could use some work, but it was so small that she wasn't sure if it even mattered. Maybe a shrub. A shrub and a lawn gnome.

"The owner of the house lives next door," Mary Beth said, gamely ignoring her mother's attitude. "He's very quiet."

"What does he do?" Lindsey's father had his measuring tape out, ready to assess.

"He's an artist."

Lindsey's mother's eyes lit up, then down. "Oh?" Her mother had some artist friends in Taos. Lindsey imagined she was concerned about her daughter living next door to a free-spirited, bad-at-responsibility guy. What kind of bad influence would he be on her impressionable daughter? Her impressionable, twenty-six-year-old, professional nurse daughter who had repeatedly demonstrated her sound and responsible judgment?

But that's what happens when you grow up in the bosom of a tight-knit family, Lindsey mused, and never leave that bosom. Her mom had spent so much time thinking she was making Lindsey's decisions for her, she didn't realize Lindsey had been perfectly capable of making her own.

Bad decisions aside, a free-spirited artist sounded kind of cool. Not at all what she was expecting from small-town Kentucky.

Good. She was ready to be surprised by life. That was why she was doing this.

"He keeps to himself," Mary Beth said. "I think he converted the garage into a studio."

"You think?" her mother asked. Lindsey pursed her lips to keep her eyes from rolling.

"Well, like I said, he keeps to himself. I don't think anyone but he has actually been in there."

"I don't like the sound of that . . ." Lindsey's dad began.

"Oh, he's perfectly safe. And very nice. I've known him for a while." Lindsey hadn't known Mary Beth for long, but she recognized a fib when she heard one. "He's just kind of secretive about his work."

"I don't like the sound of that, either," Lindsey's mom muttered, and Lindsey did roll her eyes this time. Because she knew her mom didn't mind that the guy was secretive; she didn't like the fact that her daughter was impossible to keep secrets from.

So what if Lindsey had dogged determination and unflinching curiosity? Wasn't that part of her charm?

Even if the enticement of a mysterious garage artist hadn't been there, when Lindsey walked in, she knew this was the place for her.

The hardwood floors were old, but in pretty good shape, and just begging for a small, bright area rug. The walls were a pleasant, neutral color—eggshell, if she remembered her paint samples correctly. Not very exciting for an artist's apartment, but serviceable for an artist's tenant. Besides, she was no artist. The living room and kitchen were divided by a half-wall that also served as a very charming breakfast bar. Upstairs was a good-sized bedroom with a giant closet (yay), and a bathroom with a giant claw-foot tub (YAY). Mary Beth pointed out the laundry room downstairs—not coin-operated, Lindsey was very pleased to see. Laundry "room" may have been generous, but there was enough room for the washer and dryer and a small shelving unit, and it apparently had its own closet.

Her dad tried the door. "Locked. What's in here?"

"Oh, that leads next door to Walker's apartment. The landlord."

Her mother's eyebrows shot up in alarm.

"It stays locked," Mary Beth reassured her. "And you can keep the chain on. Walker insists he's never used that door. It's just one of those peculiar things in an old house."

"That's perfect for you, Lindsey. You and your peculiar old houses."

Her mom was still a little sore that Lindsey hadn't gone for the newer, modern apartment building. But it had no character, and it was awfully close to campus. Lindsey got the feeling she would be the oldest tenant there. And then there was the sharp smell of someone smoking something that was not legal to be smoking in Kentucky. Mary Beth, whose husband was the Willow Springs Chief of Police, had rushed them out of there pretty quickly. It was pretty much the only reason Lindsey's mom hadn't gone out and signed the lease for her right then and there. Even though Lindsey was an adult and could make decisions on her own, Mom.

Lindsey did love a peculiar old house. Especially because this one was so different from the modern houses of their neighborhood outside of Phoenix, the McMansions, with their high ceilings and big, blank walls. This Kentucky house was humble and, divided in half, felt cozy.

These things were great, but Lindsey was really sold by two features: the fireplace in the living room, which reminded her that she was at last going to live in a place with seasons, and the view from the kitchen window out onto a small deck and a big backyard.

It looked like there was some semblance of a garden in the backyard. Lindsey had always wanted to try gardening, and this one looked like it could use some work. Mary Beth told them that the garden was the bailiwick of the previous tenant, and she was sure she would be able to convince Walker to let her try to restore it.

"Tomatoes," Lindsey said dreamily.

"You have to admit," her dad said to her mom, "the place does seem to suit her."

They followed MB out into the yard to get a closer look at the future home of Lindsey's tomatoes. And, though Lindsey kept this thought to herself, to sneak a peek at the garage-studio behind the overgrown garden.

Walker kicked the mud off his boots as he entered the pass code, then stepped back as the garage door opened. His eyes took a moment to adjust to the dim light, but he didn't turn the overheads on. It was sunny out, which was a nice change after a week of rain. He wanted to use the natural light today, and stepped carefully toward the curtains covering the big window. He took another grateful moment to appreciate this weirdly laid-out property, and the peculiarities of the previous owners. Who put big windows in a garage? Besides someone who wanted to convert it to an art studio.

Thank goodness for weirdos.

Before he could completely throw back the curtains, though, a movement in the yard stopped him.

People.

Oh, right.

Mary Beth had left him a message saying she was going to show Myron's apartment. He hadn't called her back, but they had already established that if he had a problem, he'd call. If not, assume it was okay.

Which worked great when he didn't forget about appointments.

He didn't need to meet the new tenants, anyway. He trusted Mary Beth's judgment. He trusted her to find someone quiet; beyond that, he didn't really care. He just wanted them to pay their rent and leave him alone.

Mary Beth told him that she was not comfortable with that level of responsibility, so he compromised: if he were home, he'd meet the tenant.

He shut the curtains.

He was not a petulant misanthrope, he reminded himself.

Despite what Myron said.

He just didn't like meeting people, not if he didn't have to. What was the point? These people might not even move in and then he would've wasted precious facial muscles forming a smile he did not mean.

But maybe they would move in. That piqued his curiosity. Not enough to go out and meet them, but enough to peek out the corner of the window.

He recognized MB, wearing those ridiculous high heels of hers, leading a middle-aged couple down the deck stairs to the yard. The woman followed closely behind MB, her mouth pinched in disapproval. Probably at the mess that was left of Myron's garden. So Walker wasn't good with actual plants. What was he going to do, pave over it?

He tried not to picture Myron's reaction to that.

The man of the couple paused on the middle step and jiggled the handrail. Walker knew it was solid—he had reinforced it a few months ago, when he thought Myron would be staying. Apparently, the guy was satisfied because he followed his wife into the yard, all while fiddling with a measuring tape.

He was so distracted by the couple's interaction that he didn't see her come out of the house at first.

She was small. When she got down the steps to stand next to MB, she was the shorter of the two. And she was curvy, which he knew because the wind picked up and pressed her flowy sundress against her body. It also blew her long, brown hair into a tangle, and Walker watched, impressed, as she pulled the mass over her shoulder and twisted it into a quick braid.

Three was kind of a crowd for that apartment. But he trusted MB, so either they were an exceptionally quiet family—unlikely, as the daughter's laugh echoed through the yard—or the parents were helping the daughter pick out housing. Which was kind of weird, since she looked like an adult. Maybe they were one of those families who did everything together, and the daughter's best friend was her mother. As if to confirm that, the daughter put her arm through her mother's and rested her head on her shoulder. The mother's pinched expression relaxed a little.

He was going to be living next to Pollyanna.

Sexy Pollyanna.

He let the curtain drop.

He had never seen so many people at the house before. It was exciting. He could just imagine how interesting all of those feet would smell. The thought set his tail wagging, and it almost set his legs jumping, but he held back. Sometimes people weren't very nice, and they made him stay locked up in a tight spot and he was not going there again. He would just stay hidden beside the little house, let his tail wag free, and bide his time. He could go out again later, when all the people had gone.

Chapter 2

Maybe it was crazy to sign a lease and move in without seeing the landlord with whom she would be sharing walls. It was almost definitely crazy, but the fact that her mother was telling her that was not helping.

"You still haven't met him? Honey, it's been almost a week."

Lindsey thought about lying, telling her mother that, yes, she had met him and he was very nice and not a serial killer at all. But she was mature enough to tell her mother the truth, and she needed her mother to accept that Lindsey was mature enough to handle her own life.

"Technically, it has only been three days, which is less than half a week and so not really *almost* a week at all."

Because Lindsey was totally mature.

"I just wonder what kind of guy rents half of his house to a single woman, that's all."

"First of all, Mom, this house is a duplex. It's two apartments. It has separate entrances. I can't even hear him through the walls. Anyway, the previous tenant was an old man, not a hot and vulnerable idiot woman like me."

"Lindsey."

"I know, I know. You trust my judgment. Despite all evidence to the contrary."

Her mother sighed. "What happened to the old man?" she asked, and Lindsey was impressed with how deftly she changed the subject.

"He had some health problems and moved in with his daughter in Ohio."

"And how did you get to the bottom of that situation?"

"I just asked Mary Beth."

"So conventional. You're losing your touch, Linds."

"Well, I thought about pulling up the floors to make sure there wasn't a body buried underneath the house, but asking seemed more efficient."

"You really are growing up, aren't you?"

"Ha ha."

"I just think it's odd that you haven't met this Walker fellow, that's all."

"He's just quiet. And he's busy. He's an artist. He probably has a show coming up."

"And you're not the least bit curious? You?"

Lindsey knew her mother was teasing, but also that she was not. She would be uneasy until she had confirmation that her daughter was not living next to a convicted serial killer, and this wouldn't be the first time she'd used Lindsey's nosiness to get the scoop for herself.

It was bad enough that, the night before her parents left to fly back to Phoenix, they sat her down and had a Serious Conversation about how they were proud of her and they knew she wanted to spread her wings a little, but wouldn't she prefer if they put a down payment on a condo in Phoenix to tide her over until she could find a job a little closer to home?

She didn't. She expressed her gratitude—again—after they helped her unload all the stuff stuffed in her hatchback into her new, cute apartment, and she got them safely to the airport. Then she went home to the fireplace and the shabby garden and the mysterious neighbor.

It wasn't that Lindsey wasn't curious. That was why she had Googled Walker Smith before she had even unpacked her underwear. And, of course, went right to the images.

There were a lot of Walker Smiths, none of whom fit the criteria she got from Mary Beth. So Lindsey used skills honed by years of insatiable curiosity (*not* stalking) and searched for "Walker Smith, Kentucky." The search results didn't include any people at all. Instead, there were pictures of metal sculptures, harsh-looking landscapes jutting from gallery walls. Kind of cool. But not really an insight into the guy next door.

"I don't know about this, Linds . . ."

Lindsey could sense that her mother was about to go into one of her here's-how-I'd-handle-the-situation speeches, which were really this-is-what-I-expect-you-to-do speeches. Logic was no match for her mother's well-meaning paranoia, as Lindsey knew. She tried for redirection.

"Hey, remember that church across the street?"

"Are they snake handlers? I knew it."

Oh my god, Lindsey thought. I am never letting her back to Kentucky. She'll offend everyone.

Or she should come here more often to get rid of some of those ridiculous stereotypes she was harboring.

No, probably better just to keep her out of the state.

"It's not a church at all. It's an antique store."

That was a little generous, but "junk shop" didn't sound like the kind of thing that would calm her mother down.

"I found the cutest couch. It's blue! Blue velvet!"

"What? Lindsey! We told you we would buy you furniture!"

"Okay, well, you can send me fifty bucks."

Her mother sighed. Again. "Well, at least it was a bargain."

"Delivery included."

"That's big of them. Across the street. Are you sure you can trust those delivery people?"

"Mom!"

"Fine. I just worry about you being murdered in your sleep."

The thought had crossed Lindsey's mind—however much she did not want to admit it, she was her mother's daughter. But Lindsey had checked and double checked the locks, used the chains on both the front and the back doors, and even went over the shared wall, looking for holes.

She was definitely her mother's daughter.

But she was confident that this place was safe, and that if it wasn't, she could take care of herself. She had mace, she knew self-defense, and she had the wife of the chief of police on speed dial.

"Anyway, I called to tell you about my first day at work."

"Oh, yes!" her mother said with suspicious nonchalance. "I forgot that was today! How did it go? What did you wear?"

Lindsey laughed. "It was great. I wore scrubs."

"I hope nobody there is too old."

"Well, Mom, it's a nursing home, so there are a few senior citizens."

"I don't know how you can work in a place like that. It's so depressing."

"This place is nice. There are only about two dozen residents, and the two nurses I'm overseeing have a lot of experience. Besides, when you're old and decrepit, don't you want someone like me taking care of you?"

"I better have *you* taking care of me when I'm old and decrepit. And you better not move me to Kentucky."

Lindsey lay back on the floor and put her feet up on the plastic tote she was using as a temporary coffee table. Despite her sensible nurse shoes, spending all day on her feet yesterday was catching up to her. That, and moving halfway across the country, apartment hunting, and then sleeping on an air mattress. Her bed, supposedly, was being delivered this afternoon. A gift from her parents.

Lindsey was not too independent to turn down some of their generosity. Not yet, at least.

She said good-bye to her mother, then let her arms fall out wide on the floor and listened to the sound of the rain pattering outside. And in about five seconds, she was asleep.

Walker pulled up the long drive to the Shady Grove Nursing Home, cursing the rain. He had hoped it would clear up enough for Myron and him to take a walk. He knew the man didn't get enough exercise, but he also knew walking on slick sidewalks was not a great idea.

So he'd sit with Myron in the sunroom and watch all the old ladies flirt with him and listen to all the gossip. For a small nursing home, a surprising amount of drama went down. Last week, Eugene May had staked his claim on Dolores Harper, even though he knew Myron had his eye on her. Walker wasn't really sure what kind of claim a man in his mid-eighties could stake, and he was fairly certain he didn't want to know. He just knew Dolores was a sweet woman, and deaf, which was probably why she liked Eugene so much. And Walker didn't say that just because he was Myron's arch-rival. The guy was pretty annoying.

He just hoped it wasn't arts and crafts day. He still had a Popsicle stick-and-pom–pom crucifix that Gladys Kilburn had made for him a few months ago, and he felt too guilty to throw it out. Then Eugene had to open his big mouth and tell the volunteer leading the class that Walker was an artist ("big-time artist" was the phrase he'd used), and the poor woman wouldn't stop deferring to Walker for his opinion on her methodology. He didn't want to hurt her feelings, but his medium was metal, not pom-poms.

The whole thing was just all-around awkward, and Walker kind of wanted to turn around and go home to avoid it. But his new tenant was home, and he was avoiding Pollyanna too. So far she had knocked on his door at least once a day, and on the garage door just as often. She left him a plate of brownies on the porch, which an animal must have gotten into. That, or she left him a plate of half-eaten brownies.

It was too bad. They looked really good.

Who was he kidding? He just ripped off any part that looked chewed, and had himself brownie for dinner.

He should just meet her and get it over with. She had signed a one-year lease, so it was unlikely that she was going anywhere. But the more he didn't meet her, the bigger a deal it seemed, and even though it had only been a few days, he felt too much pressure, like his image as a landlord must have gotten so built up in her mind that there was no way he could live up to it. And what would he say to her, anyway? "Hi, I'm Walker, and I hope to talk to you as little as possible. Welcome to Kentucky."

That might get her to stop knocking on his door.

Or he could just move in with Myron. Walker was starting to get gray hair. Maybe they would relax the age requirement. He could teach art.

A knock on his window made him jump.

"Hi, Walker!" Gladys shouted through the glass. Evan, one of the nurses, waved to him meekly from beside her where he held a large golf umbrella over both of their heads.

Walker rolled his window down. "Hi, Miss Gladys."

"I was just thinking the other day—do you remember that crucifix I made you?"

"Sure."

"Well, do you think you could bring it back the next time you come visit Myron? I want to send it to my great niece. She's getting married."

"Oh, that will be very nice."

"Okay, come on, Miss Gladys. Let's get you in out of the rain," said Evan. "Walker, Myron will be glad to see you. He's feeling a little down."

Crap. Walker rolled up his window, then climbed out of the truck. He pulled his collar up, as if that would keep him dry, and sprinted through the parking lot. He held the door open for Gladys and Evan, receiving a pinch on his cheek for his trouble.

He didn't like to think that Myron was down. Myron was his friend, and a damn good man. Plus, it made Walker feel guilty. Sure, it wasn't Walker's fault that Myron needed assisted living. Even though Walker knew he would not have been able to take care of Myron like he needed to be taken care of, even though Walker knew that Myron sometimes got down before he moved into Shady Grove, Walker still felt like there was something he should be doing to make it better.

Short of actually stopping time, Walker didn't think there was really anything he could do.

Well, he could make sure Myron didn't throw the computer out the window.

"This goddamn piece of junk!" Myron shouted, slamming the mouse down on the desk.

"What did that thing ever do to you?"

Myron looked up at Walker and his eyes softened. But just for a second. "This damn thing is eating my homework."

That was new.

"Tommy's having trouble with his Pinewood Derby car. He's sending me a picture, but the damn thing won't open!"

"Are you sure? Let me see—"

"I'm following the exact instructions that librarian gave me. What's the point of a class about email if we can't even get our emails?"

Walker clicked on the attachment. It didn't open.

"Oh, look. It doesn't open for you, either."

"Hey Myron. You almost done with that computer?" Eugene approached them. Great, Walker thought. Just what we need.

"Why, you got a hot date on the internet?"

"None of your business!"

"You can have it as soon as I get this damn file open."

"Let me see." For an old guy, Eugene was pretty strong, and he managed to push Walker out of the way and Myron out of his seat. He took the mouse and, with several deft clicks, had the image of a child's plan for a racecar on the screen.

"How did you—" Walker started.

"Now, see if you can print it, Einstein," Myron said.

The printer whirred.

Walker fetched the page. It was perfect.

"You're welcome!" said Eugene to Myron's back.

"So," said Walker, following Myron to a large table in the sunroom. "What's going on?"

"No, this is all wrong," said Myron to the paper. "No wonder this thing won't run. Look at those wheels." Walker looked. Looked like wooden wheels. "He's hardly sanded them at all. And he must have used the coarse stuff. Dammit, I told him he needed to use fine grade if he wants to get any speed on those wheels! I gotta call him. Give me your phone."

Walker patted his pockets. "Phone's in the car."

"Dammit." Myron slapped the table. "What am I gonna do with this kid?"

"Myron," Walker started. But then he didn't know how to finish. He thought Myron's temper was about more than the car, and that the conversation would require some emotional sensitivity and insight.

Walker had left that in the car, too.

"Ah, sorry, kid." Myron took pity on him. He slapped Walker on the back. "I just get upset when I see kids messing up real simple stuff."

"I remember." Walker had, once or twice, been on the receiving end of Myron's "upset." When he was the shop teacher at Willow Springs High, Myron's temper was legendary. But Walker found that, beneath all that bluster, there was a lot to learn from him.

Afternoons after school in the classroom with Myron Harris were one of his few fond memories of adolescence. Myron would be grading projects or giving detention and Walker would just tinker. That shop was where he first worked with metal. He would work, and Myron would work, occasionally offering tips or criticism, but never making him feel like he wasn't supposed to be there. It was a refuge for a skinny kid with no friends and a relief to find a creative outlet that had nothing to do with his crappy dad. But the time was far too brief. He was only in Willow Springs for a year, and then it was time to move on again.

But later, when Walker had saved enough to buy a house, he knew where he wanted to go. Willow Springs was affordable, the people were nice, and he had kept in touch with Myron, even after he retired. It seemed as good a place as any.

Myron had actually lived in the duplex next door before he bought the house. In fact, Walker was convinced that he got a good price to make up for having to deal with such a cranky tenant. But he and Myron got along great, like they always had. They left each other alone, until they didn't.

And now Myron lived in a nursing home, and Walker had rented the apartment out to Pollyanna.

He ran out to the car for his phone, brought it back into the home, and listened as Myron taught his grandson the proper way to make a wooden speed racer.

It was so quiet in the house. For the past few days, there had been only two people—the big one and the small one. The small one sure made a lot of noise. And she was outside a lot, playing in his garden. She didn't even use her paws, just a sharp, shiny thing that flung dirt everywhere. At least now it was raining, which meant she would stay inside. He huddled in his spot under the porch, where it was nice and dry. Except the spot seemed to be getting smaller. So were the holes in the fence. If they got too small, he wouldn't be able to sneak in and out. He'd be stuck in this yard, with just these two people.

Oh, well. The dirt smelled good, and it was dry. He listened to the rain fall, and closed his eyes.

Chapter 3

Weather! So far that was Lindsey's favorite thing about Kentucky, after the really nice people, the total lack of traffic, and the biscuits. Yesterday had been overcast and rainy, and she was stiff from falling asleep on the floor (which she blamed on the nap-inducing gloomy weather). Today was hot and sunny, like she was used to, but it was also humid, which she was not. Like, inside someone's mouth humid. Her hair was a frizzy mess that no ponytail could contain, and she was afraid to get up from the plastic chair on her front porch, lest she leave half of the back of her thigh on it.

Even as she sweated—just from sitting! And it wasn't even really that hot out!—she appreciated the variety. Arizona was hot and dry all the time. And even though her parents' friends told her she would hate the humidity, Lindsey wasn't there yet. Probably by the end of the summer, but for now, she was still loving it.

It was just the right amount of change, just what she'd been looking for. She didn't want to climb mountains or shave her head. She just wanted something . . . different. Different from the life she'd always had: nice weather, great parents, lovely friends she'd known forever. It was all nice. Nothing to complain about.

But it wasn't *enough*. And Lindsey thought that if she just shook things up a little, she'd get out of the rut she was feeling.

If that didn't work, she'd shave her head.

That would solve the frizz problem, at least.

For now, she had to be satisfied with sitting on her porch, sticking to her chair and thinking about how, in a few months, she'd be shoveling snow. She'd never shoveled snow before. She propped her flip-flopped feet on the porch rail and sipped her iced tea.

She felt like a real Southerner, sipping tea on the porch. Not sweet tea, though—that had been a real surprise yesterday when she went to the diner for lunch. When they called it sweet tea, they really meant it. She'd had to chase it with about a gallon of water, it was so sugary. Now she was rocking her favorite decaf blend, brewed in the sun. Her fancy artisanal iced tea, at least, was one holdover from her old life she wasn't going to get rid of any time soon. She was about to call her mom to tell her that, but then she remembered it was two hours earlier in Arizona and Mom never got up before nine on the weekend unless it was an emergency.

So Lindsey took a non-emergency selfie and sent it to her. Not murdered. Awaiting couch. Drinking tea. Much love.

"Tea that good?"

She dropped her phone, embarrassed, to see Josh McGuire from the junk store pull into the driveway with his van windows down. He slowed, and the van backfired, sending Lindsey's tea all over the porch.

"Yup." She smiled, wiping her hand on her shorts. "Want some?"

"Sure." She ran inside to get him a glass, and when she came out, he'd taken up residence on the other plastic chair. "Nothing like tea on a hot day, huh?" he asked, taking the glass from her.

He took a sip. Then sputtered all over the porch.

"Sorry," he said, wiping his mouth. "I was expecting sweet tea."

"I'm working up to it. This is just regular old perfect sun tea."

He gamely took another sip. "Mmm." He raised his glass to her, then set it on the porch. "Dad and I loaded the van last night. I'm just waiting for him so we can unload it. I don't suppose you've seen his truck, have you?" Dad was Sam McGuire, who allegedly ran the junk store. From what Lindsey had seen, Josh did most of the running.

"No, although to be fair, I'm not sure I would recognize it."

"It's red with green flames on the side."

"Ah. No, I haven't seen that one."

She saw, rather than heard, Josh curse under his breath. "Sorry. The couch will have to wait until I can track him down." He pulled out his phone and started down the porch steps.

"Oh." Lindsey pretended not to be disappointed. But tomorrow she started her first full week of work, and she was really looking forward to having some furniture before she did. She was really looking forward to the couch. "I can help you move it."

Josh took in her flip-flops and shorts. He looked skeptical.

"I'm stronger than I look," she said, which wasn't saying much since she knew she didn't look strong at all. But how bad could it be? There were about three steps from the van to the porch, then three steps up, then two steps to the living room. Nothing was so heavy that she couldn't carry it for eight steps.

He shrugged and opened the back of the van.

And there it was, in all of its tacky, plush glory.

Lindsey had never considered herself the kind of gal to go for bold furniture choices. It was kind of a commitment, no matter how appealing the red floral armchair or bright yellow coffee table looked in the catalog.

Then she moved to Kentucky, where she was Doing Things Differently. She had a neutral-walled apartment, and lived across from a store that sold blue velvet couches in excellent condition for fifty bucks because no one else wanted them.

Sure, she'd have to give it a cleaning, and she was pretty committed to removing the gold tassel border—she was going for funky chic, not brothel chic. But as she admired it, even in the poor lighting of the delivery van, she knew she'd made the right choice.

Fifteen minutes later, after she and Josh finally got all four legs out of the truck, she started reconsidering.

Walker woke up to the sky falling.

He jumped off the couch, tripping over his discarded jeans and work boots, and cursed as he landed hard on his knee. Dammit, the sky had better be falling, he said to himself as he limped to the window, or I just broke my damn knee for nothing.

He cursed under his breath when he saw it was just Sam's junk store pickup. Josh was climbing out, looking embarrassed as Lindsey approached him. They talked a while, Josh blushed, and they waved their hands and scratched their heads at whatever was in the back of the van.

Walker didn't care. He stumbled back to the couch and closed his eyes.

God, he was tired.

That was because of yesterday. After he and Myron figured out the wooden racecar—and communicated the problems to Myron's daughter—they'd gone out to lunch. Afterward, the rain had finally stopped and it was warmer than it had been when they had left. Myron was tired, so Walker took him home. "Put him down for a nap," as Myron said. But Walker hadn't been tired, and the warmth was creating a fog in the valley, so he drove up to the state forest and hiked. It was slow going because of the mud, but once he got to the top of his favorite trail, he knew it was worth it. Standing on the rocky outcrop, overlooking the green valley dotted with spots of fog, he let go of all the tension he'd been holding onto since Pollyanna had moved in next door.

The more he looked out over the valley, the more the vision for his next project solidified. He had the scrap metal, and he'd been trying to work it into a landscape, the way he'd been doing for the past year or so with other views. But standing there, free from the petty anxieties of his real life, he breathed in the humid Kentucky air and closed his eyes. When he opened them, his gaze automatically zeroed in on one tree growing out of a rocky outcrop several yards below. Well, the tree had been growing—it looked like it was dead now, with no leaves, unlike any of its neighbors.

He spent a good half hour on top of the rocks, studying the tree. Finally, he snapped a few pictures with his phone so he'd remember the shape and placement. Then he knew he needed a closer look at what bark was left, and what he could use to recreate it.

Instead of taking the safe approach, like a smart person would have done even though it involved hiking back down the trail for about half a mile, Walker decided to off-road it. Which meant he spent ninety percent of the journey down the hill on his ass. He ended up having to stop himself with his boots on the trunk of the tree— good thing it was not so dead that it was ready to fall out of the rock.

Elevation could play tricks with perspective, and up close, it was even better than he imagined. It looked like the tree had survived a fire, and died of barren old age. Its roots had split the rock, and snaked out over the edge like a claw. The branches ended in sharp fingers reaching to pinch the clouds. There were more textures on the trunk—half-dead moss, sharp bits of bark, and bare patches where an animal had taken a bite. An animal or Mother Nature. Either way, he leaned in to get a picture . . . only to find that he had cracked the screen on his phone and it wouldn't work.

He had to fight really hard to keep all of the outside crap from rushing back in then.

Instead, he took a deep breath and spent some time in front of the tree, running his hands over its shape, pocketing a piece of bark. Before he knew it, the sun was going down, and Walker knew he had to head back home. He was more careful on the way back to the trail. He didn't have a working phone—not that he got any reception in the woods. He jogged most of the way back to the truck and scrambled for the sketchpad he kept under the seat. With a few frantic swipes of his pencil, he had the rough shape of the tree down, then made some quick close-up sketches of the trunk. Satisfied that he wouldn't totally forget everything when he got home, he tossed a towel on the driver's seat to keep the mud off and headed home.

The problem with being struck by inspiration was that it totally interfered with Walker's sleep, which was not a great thing when working with welding tools and industrial epoxy. Still, it was the wee hours of the morning before Walker stumbled inside and kicked off his muddy clothes and collapsed in a heap on the couch. His eyes were bleary from experimenting with detailed texturing, but his brain was still wired.

So Walker turned to the only thing that consistently worked to cure his insomnia, a trick he'd picked up in fourth grade, his first time in foster care. He was staying with the Garcias, a big, raucous Cuban family in North Carolina. He would come home after school and sit with Abuelo Hector while he watched his stories. There was something about the rhythm of the fight music and the love music and the happy music and the sad music that never failed to lull him to sleep. So that night—that morning—he turned on the one Spanish channel in Willow Springs, and before he could say *buenas noches*, he was asleep.

Until, a sad few hours later, Josh's damn truck backfired and woke him up.

This neighbor was trouble.

And it sounded like she and Josh were trying to knock down the damn house. Walker was just drifting off to sleep again when he heard Josh curse and Pollyanna scream, and a loud thump and more cursing, and dammit, Walker was awake now.

First, some of the gold fringe ripped off when they were maneuvering the couch out of the truck. That was no big deal, since Lindsey had planned to remove the fringe anyway. The couch was from the sixties or seventies, and, as Sam had pointed out to her, they didn't make furniture like that anymore. With proper care, it would last another thirty or forty years. It was made of sturdy stuff.

Also: heavy stuff.

Lindsey started behind the dolly, standing on the metal bridge thing that Josh had pulled out and run across to the porch. When it became clear that this would mean Lindsey would be, essentially, catching the couch, they switched places. Lindsey leaned into it, it hit the dolly, and Josh muscled it over the bridge to the porch. He maneuvered like a pro, and Lindsey was duly impressed. When she told him so, he blushed, which she thought was sweet. Of course, it was possible the blush was just heatstroke.

From here on out it was smooth sailing, Josh panted. Just over the lip in the doorway, then just put 'er inside, then set on the porch and have some more of Lindsey's weird tea.

Unfortunately, in addition to being sturdy, the couch was also huge. When she'd discovered it, Lindsey felt its size was only secondary in wonderfulness to its style. She could just picture it: come home after a long shift, stretch out on the couch, and slowly get back to life. Or, more likely, fall asleep watching a reality TV marathon. Either way, there would be wine involved, and the amazing comfort of an oversized blue velvet couch.

She had not really considered getting the couch through the front door.

Josh gamely checked to see if maybe, somehow, they had overlooked that this couch came in pieces, or if the back door was wider than the front. But Lindsey's dad had measured. Both doors were the same size, which was just about the width of the couch. They were going to have to muscle it in. Hopefully the plushness would give enough so they could push it inside, Josh suggested. He looked worried, then he looked for detachable pieces. The feet came off, which gave them a few inches.

Unfortunately, this was just enough space to trick them into thinking they would make it.

"Maybe the arms come off?" Josh started fiddling with the upholstery.

Lindsey was seriously regretting her impulsive purchase—maybe inflatable furniture would come back in style. Was it ever in style? It was hard to think about those things when she was busting a vein trying to maneuver her dream couch inside the front door. Stupid dreams.

Josh was out on the porch, wiping his sweat on his T-shirt, while Lindsey grabbed an arm and leaned her entire body weight back.

The couch remained unmoved.

Rather than risk a hernia, she thought if she and Josh switched places, that might work. He helped her climb over and between, then hoisted himself over and assumed the position. He gave the word, and she threw her weight against the couch . . . which still didn't move.

"Hold on, we need to come in at an angle."

"How is there an angle that can make this work?" Lindsey didn't mean to sound petulant, but with every gut-busting shove, she felt her dream couch slip away.

Which at this point would have been a nice change from the way it was now stuck in the doorway.

"Okay, I got it. You go this way and I'll go that way. Go!"

Lindsey pulled, getting down low into a squat to get her legs more involved. She grunted and squealed and it moved, just a little, but she didn't hear Josh stop pushing and her squat went all wonky and before she knew it, she was going down in one of those slow motion disasters that you experience with enough clarity to realize what is going on, even though it's happening too fast to stop it. So she landed, butt on the porch, then gravity tipped her back and then her legs were over her head and she tumbled down the steps, landing on her back with a stunned *huff*.

"Holy crap! Lindsey!" Then Josh was in her face, looking ready to do CPR.

She waved him away. "I'm fine." She coughed, and started to stand. He grabbed her under the elbow and started to help her up while she righted her clothes, causing even more of a tangle, and taking Josh down with her. She laughed, then looked sadly at her new front door/dream couch.

Before she could despair completely, though, there was a bang. And then: whoa.

Walker—she assumed it was Walker, since the man emerged from the apartment next door—looked pissed. Also, ripped. Two sides of her brain fought for attention. The first was wondering what kind of man sat around in just his boxer shorts in the middle of the day. The second, and the one that was frankly winning the fight, was admiring those boxer-clad thighs, and was just starting to move on to the perfect ratio of chest hair to muscle definition. But as quickly as the Angry Adonis had appeared, he was gone, leaving just the echo of a door slam in his wake.

Lindsey finished her scramble, realizing that gawping with her legs askew was probably not the most favorable first impression to make on a guy. By the time she was upright, Angry Adonis was back. This time he was wearing jeans and a T-shirt (boo, said her brain) (and other parts of her body), and she was just about to introduce herself and apologize for disturbing him when he glared at Josh, who apparently understood angry-man looks because he scrambled up and over the couch. Walker proceeded to lift the end of the couch that had so recently bested her, and with a series of grunts that apparently only men could understand, he and Josh had turned the couch sideways, then up, then down, then at more complicated angles that Lindsey could not keep up with (he was wearing a shirt, but she could still admire the muscles in his back—distracting!), and the couch was inside.

There was a "thank you" on the tip of her tongue, and an offer of coffee or tea or me, but Walker just looked at her, shook his head, and slammed back into his house.

This was going to be interesting, she thought as she climbed up the steps and into her living room. So much for a pleasant landlord/tenant relationship. First she woke him from apparent hibernation, then she ogled him, then she pressed him into manual labor.

Then she looked at the couch, which was the perfect touch of decadence and whimsy in her otherwise sensible living room, and she thought, forget it. She could deal with a hostile neighbor. She wasn't moving.

Too much work.

The noise woke him up from his nap, but that was okay. He shouldn't have been sleeping anyway. He thought about coming out from under the porch, barking and announcing his intentions, which were to receive love and snacks. But then there was another noise, and it reminded him of the place he'd left, where doors slammed and, if he wasn't fast, his tail got caught. But he was still curious, so he snuck out to the front where he watched the people fight with something big and soft that he wanted to sleep on. They looked like they were having fun, and he wanted to join in, especially when the lady tumbled on the ground. She was so close to him! He wanted to run over and lick her face!

But then the door slammed again and he didn't stick around to hear what it was.

Chapter 4

"You got a burr under your tail?"

Myron barely looked at Walker as he reached for the paper bag on Walker's lap. Walker held on to it and handed Myron his turkey-on-wheat-no-mayo. Walker knew from experience that if he didn't hold on to his own double-stacked roast beef, he'd lose it. Myron was quick for an old guy, as he liked to say, and Walker wasn't exactly firing on all cylinders this morning.

"No. I came to see you, didn't I?"

"Yeah, this has been a real blast. You barely say two words when you come to pick me up, and then you insist on signing me out like a wimp."

"You're supposed to sign out when you leave."

"Rules! Rules were meant to be broken! You're too young to forget about that."

"Last time we broke out, you lost your Bingo privileges."

"Oh, yeah. Broke my heart. I lost my chance to win a bag of sugar-free hard candies. Those things aren't worth putting in my dentures for."

Walker just shrugged and bit into his sandwich. It was salty and juicy, which was just what he needed after a night of no sleep. He was getting old. He used to be able to stay up all night, no problem. Now he felt like he had a hangover.

"So who pissed in your Cheerios?"

Walker almost choked on his sandwich. "Colorful," he said around a mouthful of beef.

"You've had that assy face on since you came to pick me up. Now, I know I ain't always the greatest company, but usually you at least pretend to be glad to see me."

"It's nothing. I just didn't get a lot of sleep last night." He stuffed his now empty sandwich wrapper back into the bag, dug out the homemade pickle.

Myron's eyes lit up. "New project?"

Walker thought about Lindsey smiling, and struggling with the couch, and laughing with Josh. "Something like that."

"Well, good." Myron wrapped the uneaten half of his sandwich and put it in his coat pocket. Walker made a mental note to take it out when they got back to Shady Grove.

Walker smiled. Myron was the only exception to his rule about keeping works in progress under wraps. Although he'd never admit it, Myron had a really good artistic eye. He could spot problems in perspective or composition, things that would sometimes plague Walker that he couldn't quite put his finger on.

When Myron lived next door, he'd also done a good job of keeping an eye on Walker's schedule. If Walker was still working when Myron woke up in the morning, there would be hell to pay. And then there'd be scrambled eggs.

"Can't wait to get a look at it. Fix all of your problems for you."

"That'll be nice," Walker said, before he remembered that if Myron came over, he'd probably meet Lindsey, and Lindsey was the reason he had a burr under his tail. "Ready?"

Myron nodded, then got slowly to his feet. They started their first lap around the Duck Puddle, as the folks in Willow Springs called it. This time of year it was more geese than ducks, but the path around the pond was paved and dotted with benches, so it was perfect for getting Myron some exercise.

Or "taking his old man for a walk," as Myron called it.

"But we both know that's not what you're cranky about. Out with it, son."

Once, a few months after Walker had bought the house, he had tried to hide the fact that a journalist was constantly calling, after getting his number out of an impressionable young intern at the Madison Kelly Gallery. The *New Yorker* had run a small piece about a group exhibit he had been a part of, and apparently this guy's life would not be complete without invading Walker's privacy. Or "writing an exclusive profile," as he called it. Walker called it putting him under a microscope, where everything mattered but the art.

That gave Walker major assy face.

He had tried to go about his business, fix Myron's wonky toilet and change his light bulbs without letting on that anything was bothering him. His problem had nothing to do with Myron. Myron, unlike pushy New York journalists, understood privacy and boundaries and personal space. At least, Myron acted like he understood those things.

It took about two days of gentle, but constant, prodding before Myron coaxed it out of him. Then the next time the guy called, Myron grabbed the phone (he was pretty quick for an old man, especially when Walker was caught off guard) and gave him what-for.

Actually, Myron told the guy that he had the wrong number, but while he had him on the phone, had he accepted Jesus as his personal lord and savior? And would he trust in the goodness of God to save him from the fiery sting of the rattler's venom?

The reporter never called again.

And Walker learned that it was not worth the energy trying to keep secrets from Myron. It was not the most normal way to form a friendship, going from shop teacher to guardian angel, but then what did Walker know about normal friendships?

But that didn't mean he had to like it. Not all the time, anyway.

"I have a new neighbor," he admitted as he helped Myron the rest of the way off the bench while pretending not to.

Myron pretended not to lean on Walker's arm. "What's he like? Is he cuter than me?"

Walker thought about shorts and scowls. "Yeah."

"Ah, so no chance of getting my old room back?"

Myron smiled like he was joking, but Walker knew better. He knew it killed the old man to be in a home, to have to rely on other people to take care of him. Walker hated that. Even if Lindsey were a perfect tenant—which she was not—Walker would give anything to give Myron his independence back. But the house had too many stairs, and Myron was too stubborn to see that leaving the lights on overnight was one thing, but leaving the oven on all day was another.

Shady Grove was for the best.

The best sucked.

"She's driving me crazy," he told the old man.

"She?" Myron's eyes lit up with interest.

Walker ignored the eyebrows. "She makes a lot of noise."

"With those paper-thin walls? What'd she do, sneeze?"

"And she's nosy. She keeps asking people about me."

"Probably wants to make sure you're not a serial killer. You do tend to give that first impression." Myron put a hand on Walker's arm and they stopped and sat on the next bench. "He was so quiet, they always say. We never would have guessed he was secretly chopping people up." Myron pulled the second half of his sandwich out of his pocket and began unwrapping it.

"Is she cute?" asked Myron.

"Cuter than you."

"So, very cute."

Walker sighed. "Yeah, she's cute."

Myron ripped off a corner of mayo-free bread and threw it to the ducks. "And you don't like that."

Walker didn't say anything to that.

"She married?"

Walker shook his head. At least, he didn't think she was married. If she was, she sure didn't live with her husband.

"Boyfriend?"

Walker shrugged, although he was pretty sure the answer was no, if the way she was flirting with Josh was any indication. If she did have a boyfriend, he didn't live around here. There was no way a man from around here would live in a house with a couch like that.

They got up and started walking again.

"So, you've got a cute, probably single woman living next door. She's loud and nosy, which, coming from you probably means she said 'hello' once or twice."

Walker watched the Duck Puddle. Really interesting place, the Duck Puddle.

"Does she ask you to fix things?"

"Not yet."

"So she's cute, single, polite, and so far she hasn't asked you to do your job as her landlord. Sounds terrible."

"You don't get it."

Myron reached for Walker's arm again and sat on the bench behind them. Walker sat next to him, watched him closely.

"I'm fine," said Myron, waving off Walker's concern. "But I want to make sure you're paying attention." He squeezed Walker's forearm. "I know you need to be alone to work. But you've convinced yourself that you need to be alone all the time."

"I'm not dating my tenant."

"I'm not saying you date her."

Walker raised his eyebrows at Myron's dirty mind, then quickly blinked the expression away when he realized that was not what Myron meant. He should definitely not just sleep with Lindsey. That was a ridiculous idea. Totally inappropriate.

His mind was filled with a sudden image of those shorts.

"It's not gonna kill you to be nice to her, that's all."

Walker grunted. She seemed like a nice girl. If he were nice to her, she'd be nice to him. Then she'd see that his house was a mess and his sleep was irregular and his diet was a joke and she'd try to take care of him. He didn't need a mother. Hell, he didn't even need a girlfriend. He just needed a nice, quiet tenant who left him alone and had liver spots.

His phone beeped with the alarm Walker had set so they would get back to Shady Grove on time. Good. Now Walker wouldn't have to talk about Pollyanna and her shorts. That thought immediately sent a jolt of guilt through him—what kind of guy wants to get rid of a friend because of an uncomfortable conversation?

Walker Smith: Stand-Up Guy.

"All right, all right," Myron said before Walker got the chance to say the words forming in his mouth. "I know, it's time to get back so Nurse Ratched can take her attendance and give me my pills."

Nurse Ratched was actually Molly Callahan, Shady Grove head nurse, who was in her late sixties and very nice.

"You're going to miss her when she's gone." Walker stood behind Myron as he climbed into the truck.

"She's already gone. Retirement party was last week. With my luck, she'll move in next door."

"Or the new Nurse Ratched will be even worse."

"Don't think I haven't thought about that."

Walker closed the door, shook his head, and drove Myron back to Shady Grove.

Lindsey snapped the lock shut on her new locker, reminding herself that she was an adult now. Adults sometimes had lockers. Shady Grove's owner, Ned Grubb, had told her with pride that the lockers had been salvaged from the old high school, and repainted Wildcat Blue, which was apparently the color of the University of Kentucky basketball team. Lindsey guessed that because this was the color Ned wore every day, usually in the form of a seemingly never-ending supply of polo shirts with the UK Wildcats logo emblazoned on it.

She wasn't known as Detective Lindsey for nothing.

There were still streamers up in the staff room from Molly Callahan's retirement party, but today was her first official day retired, and Lindsey's first official day as head nurse. She was a little nervous. She knew she was young, but she was qualified. She had her degree and professional experience, and she'd been working in nursing homes since she was in high school. She knew the lay of the land. She knew how to handle geriatric medicine, and how to handle geriatric emergencies. And, for extra comfort, because Kentuckians were pretty much the nicest people ever, Molly was on voluntary speed-dial for the next week until she left for her Caribbean cruise. Nothing to be nervous about. Just get briefed, then start making rounds.

Hope Neely, the overnight nurse, was at their shared desk. "It was pretty quiet last night, thank goodness," she said, knocking on the wooden desk. "Mr. May didn't want to take his blood pressure medicine, but I was able to sneak it into his ice cream."

"Clever."

"Having two kids is good training for this job."

Lindsey laughed.

"Okay. You have everyone's medical records, and I think Molly showed you the activity schedule, right?"

"The big calendar in the sunroom?"

"That's the public schedule." Hope pulled a well-used desk calendar from a drawer. "This is ours. It's a little more informative."

Lindsey thumbed through it. Today was a visit from therapy dogs, then arts and crafts later. Next week was the Bookmobile, then something she couldn't read, illustrated by what looked like dripping blood.

"What's this?" she asked, alarmed.

"That's Evan's sense of humor. Sorry about that. That day we have the middle school choir coming in to sing."

"Are they that bad?"

"I say this as a woman who has two kids in that choir: yes. But they mean well, and most of the residents like it. Sometimes the kids get weird around old people, but other than that, you'll be fine. I suggest making yourself busy in another room."

Hope grabbed her purse, and Lindsey walked with her through the common areas. Hope re-introduced her to the residents, most of whom declared that of course they remembered Lindsey, what a nice-looking young woman. There were a few jokes questioning whether or not she was old enough to administer medication, then Hope left her alone with her new charges.

"You have big shoes to fill, young lady," said an old man, crocheting in front of the unlit fireplace.

"Leave the lady alone, Eugene," said a woman playing bridge at a sunny card table. "I'm out."

Okay. Maybe that wasn't bridge.

"Thanks, Mrs. Harper," Lindsey told her. "I can handle Mr. May."

"Oh, he'll behave," said Dolores Harper. "If he knows what's good for him."

Lindsey raised her eyebrows in alarm, but Mr. May just laughed into his afghan.

The front door beeped open and Lindsey turned to see Mr. Harris slowly amble toward the group. A car squealed out of the parking lot.

"Hi, Mr. Harris," she said as she approached and gave him her arm. He looked at her, confused.

"I'm the new Nurse Ratched," she reminded him.

"Ah. Good." He patted her hand paternally. "Call me Myron. I don't like when beautiful women call me Mr. Harris. Makes me feel old."

"That's because you are old!" shouted Mr. May from the fireplace.

"So what have you been up to this afternoon?" she asked, but Myron had pulled away and embedded himself in the ladies' poker game. Good thing it was a rhetorical question—Hope told her Myron frequently went to lunch with a family friend. Still, Lindsey didn't like his lack of focus. She made a mental note to review his chart more carefully and to talk to his family about any possible memory loss.

For now, though, he seemed happy to help Gladys Kilburn cheat at cards. She left him to it.

Where did these people go all day? At first, he'd wanted the place all to himself, but now he was starting to get worried that they weren't coming back at all. Good thing his legs were fast and his nose was strong. He would find the lady, no matter where she went.

Chapter 5

Four hours of sleep. That must have been a mid-project record for him; usually he went for days on four hours of sleep. But he didn't feel refreshed or rested at all. Probably because he'd spent all night dreaming about a nurse, coming into his room and making him feel all better.

Sexy nurse dreams. Was he twelve?

The worst part was, they were not just sexy nurse dreams, no matter how much he tried to convince himself otherwise. He was having sexy nurse dreams about Pollyanna. Of course she worked with the elderly and infirm. Walker had seen her the day before when he'd dropped Myron off at Shady Grove. He saw her through the glass doors, waiting in the foyer for Myron to come in, and he peeled out of the parking lot so she wouldn't see him. So he was a total chicken, and she was freakin' Mother Teresa.

Which, unfortunately, did nothing to deter his sexy nurse dreams.

Everything about this is wrong, he told himself as he poured an extra scoop of coffee into the coffeemaker. He needed diesel fuel this morning. He needed a lobotomy. Or, he thought as he trudged upstairs to throw on some clothes, he just needed to get to work. Everyone has an inappropriate sex dream every now and then. When he was fifteen, he had a sex dream about his history teacher, who wore orthopedic shoes and cat sweaters.

She was pretty cute, though.

At least in his dream.

He didn't do so great in history that year.

It didn't matter. Mother Teresa was his tenant. She was also in charge of the care of his only friend. An entanglement with her would mean nothing but complications, and he didn't need complications.

His dealer wanted him to be part of a group show in New York, and a New York show meant he had to have new work, and new work meant he couldn't spend all night having weird sex dreams about nuns with bad taste in couches. It would take months to create the piece. Even with a clear idea of how he wanted it to look, the actual end product was up in the air. He hated that fluffy sort of artist talk, but it was true: he just had to feel it.

Before he could feel anything, though, he needed coffee.

Jeans on, boots on, mug in hand, he headed out the back door to the garage to wait for inspiration to strike.

Instead of inspiration, though, he got a dose of Mother Pollyanna in shorts and a tank top, hands on hips, glaring at the remains of Myron's garden.

She must have heard him step stealthily off the back porch (damn work boots), because she turned to him.

And smiled.

God, she had a great smile.

Walker took a sip of his coffee.

"Morning," she said. He gave a little wave and headed toward the garage.

"Oh, hey," she said, holding out a hand to stop him as he passed. "I'm really sorry about the other day. About waking you up with that couch?" she added when he looked confused.

"That's okay," he said, trying hard not to remember the different ways he had considered murdering her and Josh McGuire.

"I used to work nights. It totally messes up your sleep schedule, right? They did not make blackout curtains strong enough to convince me that it was possible for me to sleep during the day."

She was being sweet. She needed to stop being sweet. Or he needed to remember that he didn't do sweet. He liked a woman with a hard edge and a mean streak. He didn't like women who apologized for their mistakes and wore purple short-shorts.

"Anyway, I'll try to be more quiet." She gave him that million-dollar Pollyanna smile again. "I'm Lindsey, by the way."

He shook her hand, then retreated quickly to the coffee.

"You're Walker, right? I mean, I'd hate to think this whole time I've been . . ." She trailed off.

This whole time she'd been what, exactly?

"It's just funny that we haven't met since I moved in, is all. You'd think with sharing the number of walls we share that we'd run into each other more often. I guess our schedules are really different."

Walker eyed the garage door. He was so close . . .

"So . . . Mary Beth tells me you're an artist. That's so interesting. I saw some pictures of your work online but I'd love to see . . ."

He didn't hear the rest of it. He never talked about his art in progress with anyone. Anyone except Myron, and barely that. He didn't even talk anything beyond vague concepts with Madison, and she was the one who signed the checks. So he definitely wasn't going to suddenly start talking about it with Pollyanna in her purple shorts and her messy ponytail and her great legs.

He grunted, which meant good-bye, and stalked into the garage to hide from the pretty lady, and, hopefully, to get some damn work done.

Lindsey watched Walker's retreating back as he stalked into the garage. It was a nice back. The whole view was nice. Too bad he was such a . . . what was he? Maybe he just wasn't a morning person.

Or maybe he was a jerk.

She didn't like that. They didn't need to be besties, but a cordial relationship would be nice. Maybe, over time, he'd mellow out and just be unpleasant.

But, man, she wanted to get into that garage.

No. It was none of her business, and he had made it abundantly clear that she was not welcome.

Or had he? Maybe he was just shy! Maybe he'd had a rough life on the streets and didn't know how to accept people's kindness! Maybe he secretly wanted to show off his work, but his fear of rejection was so great that it paralyzed his social skills!

Or maybe he wasn't making art at all. Maybe he was making meth.

Okay. Now we're getting crazy, she told herself. Detective Lindsey could sometimes go into overdrive and become Crazy Paranoid Lindsey. What she really needed to do was respect his wishes, and if Walker came around to wanting her in his studio, he'd invite her in. She could be patient. She could wait, and she could accept that it might never happen.

She could!

That's why she was shouting at herself! Because it was totally true, and not at all because she needed convincing!

Whatever. At least she had a cute apartment, and she was getting to try her hand at gardening. As long as Walker didn't mind. She should go into the garage and ask him. *No, stop,* she told herself. *You're just being nosy. Just stalk him on the internet like a normal person.* Besides, the lease said she had access to the garden, which to her meant she could tear the whole thing up if she wanted to.

She did not. When she wasn't researching her landlord for her own peace of mind (she told herself), she'd been all over the internet looking for gardening tips. The Willow Springs Public Library had a great list of online resources that gave her hope that she wouldn't have to start the garden from scratch. In fact, that was a bad idea. She even downloaded a free gardening app that Gladys turned her on to. Since she was going to leave Walker alone, she stood there with her phone out, trying to identify various green things poking out of the dirt. According to her research, some of it might be salvageable. With her starting kind of late in the season, she wanted to save all that she could.

She practically jumped up and down with glee. Late in the season. She'd never had a season to be late in before!

It was not too late for tomatoes. Zucchini would be fine, eggplant maybe. She couldn't tell if she had melon or pumpkin, which was embarrassing, but fortunately no one was there to see her squat down and try to figure it out.

She wished she could talk to the man who'd planted the garden. She imagined he'd have some good advice for her. But more than that, the garden was clearly a labor of love. Beneath the weeds—she was pretty sure those were weeds—she could see neat rows laid out inside a border of wildflowers. She wanted to show him that, just because he'd moved away, a part of him remained in Willow Springs. Maybe, once she got it whipped into shape, she could invite him over. Make him some apparently terrible iced tea. Or maybe Walker was still in touch with him, and he could keep the guy updated. Or she could ask Walker to invite him over and the three of them could have lunch. And, if Walker spoke actual words to her, it might be more fun than a root canal. That would be an amazing step forward in their relationship.

Not that they had a relationship.

A girl could dream.

And this girl maybe did dream. About an angry man in boxers.

Oh, Lord, those boxers.

She shook her head. No. No no no no no. She was on a Fresh Path to Independence, not a Do-Dumb-Stuff-with-Your-Landlord-Even-If-It-Looks-Super-Fun Path. And taming that angry bear who lived next door would definitely be trouble. She didn't want trouble. She didn't want to reform a bad boy. That stuff was not for her. If the bad boy wanted to change, he'd change. A person can only be who he is. That's how she'd ended up getting anxiety hives when her last boyfriend talked about marriage. She was not a homebody. She was not a stay-local kind of gal, and she'd been living her whole life as if she were.

She had enough trouble trying to figure her own stuff out; she didn't need to try to figure out someone else's.

No matter how tempting it was.

No amount of head-shaking could convince her that she did not want to see what those flexing muscles looked like up close. Fortunately, he was clearly a jerk.

But what a hot jerk.

A hot jerk with a secret.

Not only was he a jerk, but he was clearly disgusted by her. Which was not really fair. He hadn't exactly seen her at her best. She looked down at her worn cotton shorts. Definitely not her best. And the last time he saw her, she was wearing different old shorts and being bested by blue velvet. But that shouldn't matter. Dad always told her not to judge a book by its cover. "Wait until someone gives you a reason to dislike 'em," he always said.

All she had to do was pay her rent and stay out of his way. What was she trying to do, sleep with him?

That had her pausing over a squash blossom.

No, of course not. That would be a terrible idea. He was her landlord. That was like sleeping with your boss, she told herself. Bad bad bad idea.

But he wasn't really her boss. What was the worst that could happen? He could evict her if it didn't work out. That would suck.

But that back. Those hands.

There were other apartments in the world.

No, no. No sleeping with Grumpy Walker. She was here to be independent, to work hard, and to make her own mistakes without a parental safety net. She had a big, demanding job that would take up all of her energy. She would be way too tired for ill-advised sex.

She also had a mess of a garden.

Lindsey bent over the plot and pulled out a weed. There were a lot of weeds. That was okay. She wasn't afraid of a few weeds. Or a few thousand weeds. She kneeled down at the edge of the plot and started pulling.

What was she doing out there? From his hiding spot under the porch, he could hear her making noises. It sounded like she was playing in his jungle. He started to wag his tail. He wanted to play with her! He started to wiggle his way under the boards, and the cold dirt floor felt so good on his belly he almost gave up his mission and sat there wiggling. But then he got a good look at what she was doing. She was pulling his jungle apart! She was tossing big green pieces over her shoulder into a pile!

Actually, that pile looked like it would be fun. He'd just wait down here until she was gone, then he'd have the pile all to himself. In the meantime, this dirt wasn't going to roll in itself . . .

Chapter 6

Lindsey woke up restless. She was a morning person, and she was used to being at her most productive when she got out of bed. But she wasn't used to feeling like this. Antsy, her old boss would have called it. She lay there, admiring the clean paint job on the ceiling, making a mental list of things to be anxious about.

Job: so far, so good. Still a lot to learn, but she was okay with that. Friends: could use some work. Mary Beth had invited her to join her book club, and this month's selection sat on her nightstand. It wasn't exactly the raucous honky-tonkin' she secretly hoped for when she moved to Kentucky, but she was willing to give that some time. Family: all in Arizona, all healthy, all starting to worry about her a little less, which was progress. Home: . . .

Maybe that was it. Despite her efforts over the past few weeks, Walker still remained a grumpy mystery. And the mystery was beginning to get really deep under her skin. She wanted to know what his deal was, and not just because she wanted to know what his deal was.

Why was he so quiet? What was his art like? Did he think she wouldn't be able to just Google him to find out? Because she had, and it was cool. Very masculine, but somehow delicate and beautiful at the same time. They were landscapes, of a sort, metal that seemed to be flat or stamped with images, but when the photographer zoomed in, it was actually shaped and . . . carved, maybe?

Of course, there was practically no information included, except that it was steel and copper, and there were six of them hanging in a gallery in New York City.

Seeing images of his work made her even more curious about him. What kind of guy has the patience and vision to create what he created?

And why did he apparently hate her?

Maybe she'd been coming on too strong. Maybe what she thought of as a normal, neighborly level of friendliness was a creepy, stalker-level invasion of privacy to him. Maybe he was sensitive. He was an artist, after all.

Right. Okay. Things looked a little brighter if she thought of her neighbor as sensitive and shy rather than a grumpy hatemonger. She could live with sensitive and shy. She would just tread a little more lightly. She'd avoid any unnecessary contact. She would let him come to her, if he wanted to. And if he didn't want to, well, that would be okay too. They would just be two strangers who inhabited the same general space but had no kind of relationship whatsoever.

She could live with that.

Ceiling and life fully examined, Lindsey hopped out of bed. She had some time before work—she could weed in the garden a little. Looking out the window, she changed her mind. She was beginning to love her garden, but not enough to work on it in a steady downpour. She was also starting to miss the desert.

She drew the curtain closed before she could notice if the light in the garage was still on, which meant that Walker either got up earlier than she did—unnatural!—or spent all night in there working, which she shouldn't notice because she was trying to keep a healthy distance from her sensitive and shy neighbor.

Who was she kidding? She had noticed. And in the time it took her to close the curtain, she considered, then rejected, bringing him a mug of coffee for energy and maybe also to enable her to sneak a peek at his work. And his shoulders. No, mostly his work.

But, no. Healthy distance. Sensitive and shy. Let him make the first platonic move, if there was a move to be made.

But since he was in the garage, that meant he wasn't in his house, which meant she wouldn't wake him up like she had all those weeks ago with The Great Couch Disaster. And as much as she would like to see him all steamy and mad in his boxers, that was not in her Healthy Distance Plan, so she banished the image (mostly) from her mind.

Exercise. She needed exercise to burn off some of this excess mental energy. Rain meant this would not be the morning she took up running—hooray. But she was well equipped to deal with unpleasant weather interrupting her exercise plans. She threw on a sports bra and a pair of shorts and padded down to the living room. This morning felt like a Bollywood Blast morning. And if Walker was in the garage, she could crank it up and sing along, which was her preferred method of Bollywood Blasting. The extra diaphragm work was good for her abs. And she was a dork who couldn't help but sing along, even though she didn't know the words, or even the language.

Whatever. Who was going to see her? She popped in the DVD and started Blast-ing.

Walker was climbing through a window and his head kept hitting wind chimes. He hated wind chimes. Only jerks put up decorations that would jangle and crash in a place where they were the only ones who could not hear it, while they sat in comfortable silence behind a door. Why were there wind chimes in his window? But then he went inside, and there were more wind chimes. And some of them had a serious bass line. He reached up, determined to rip one of those jangling death monsters out of the ceiling, when—

Walker sat up like a bolt. After a second of adjusting to reality, he rubbed his hands over his face. He had to stop falling asleep on the couch. He barely remembered stumbling through the back door, although he did recall looking in despair at the insurmountable flight of stairs leading to his bedroom.

He was acting more tortured than artist, and he was starting to piss himself off.

But the jangly bass wind chimes were not a dream, after all. They were coming through the wall. And they sounded like music. And— was that singing?

Or was someone murdering a turkey?

He weighed his options. He could ignore what he guessed was Lindsey singing and stick a pillow over his head and continue to emit only grumbles in her presence. Or he could go over and confront her, ask her nicely to turn down the music, and start to develop a civil relationship.

He looked at his pillow.

Then he heard Myron's voice in his head, telling him to "Man up. Are you afraid of one little woman?"

He wasn't afraid. Walker was not afraid of Lindsey! And she wasn't that little. She was short, but she wasn't little. She was curvy, a perfect handful . . .

Either way, he was not afraid of her.

He would go over and confront her.

Nicely.

The start of a beautiful friendship.

Lindsey was totally lost in the music, which was why she loved the Bollywood Blast routine. She could get her dance on and get her workout on at the same time. All in the privacy of her own little living room. It was very efficient.

She was feeling the bass, flicking her hips on the downbeat. First right, then turn, then left.

On the second turn-then-left, she saw a shadowy figure standing in her doorway.

She screamed.

She was so startled out of her Bollywood Blast reverie that it took her a long, screaming second to realize that the shadowy figure was Walker. And that he looked pissed.

Surprise.

"What are you—" she started as she threw the front door open. Then she watched his eyes blaze an angry trail down her body. She quickly covered up her sports bra with her hands. Then she uncovered it and put her hands on her hips. It was her apartment. She could walk around in a bra if she wanted to. Hell, she could walk around without a bra.

He shook his head, focused back on her eyes. "What the hell are you doing in here?"

"What am I—? This is my apartment! What are you doing in here?"

"Well, I *was* trying to sleep in *my* apartment, but then it sounded like someone was murdering a turkey over here, so I came over to investigate."

"No one's murdering—" Then she got it. He'd heard her singing. Ha ha ha. She was a terrible singer. She took a deep breath. He was just mad because she'd woken him up. And because he was a jerk. But in this case, his jerkitude was possibly justified. "I thought you were in the garage."

"Why would you think that? It's barely six in the morning."

"Because the light was on in there!"

She saw him pause, saw the corner of his mouth try to hitch up into a smile. "You were watching me in the garage? Are you spying on me?"

"Says the man standing in my living room. Uninvited."

She thought she saw him blush, then drop his eyes. Well, whatever. It was just a sports bra.

Oh my god, she thought. Walker is embarrassed. He was embarrassed by her sports bra! Her glee at that idea totally erased any residual embarrassment she felt at being caught singing loudly and badly in an unfamiliar foreign language.

"Can you just . . . keep it down?" he spat. "Please?"

She cocked her hip and smiled. "Since you said *please.*" Then she turned toward the kitchen. She was done with her workout. She needed a glass of water.

"Show yourself out?" she threw over her shoulder, and stuck her head in the fridge.

Boom. She heard the front door close, and smiled.

This was getting ridiculous. She wasn't *that* hot. She was . . . it probably didn't matter what she looked like. Whenever Walker saw Lindsey, he wanted to touch her. Just to see if her skin was as soft as it looked.

And . . . he was officially a creep.

It wasn't his fault that he kept running into her while she was wearing short shorts and sports bras and other things that showed off a lot of probably soft skin. Just because he always saw her in the yard or, you know, inside her own apartment. Just because this was the twenty-first century and, fine, she could wear whatever she wanted. He didn't have to like it. He didn't have to like that he liked it.

But seriously, would it kill her to put on pants?

By the time he reached the garage door, though, Walker was all out of steam. He was just going to have to accept that he was renting to a very annoying woman to whom he was unfortunately attracted. He would have to get Mary Beth to help him re-word the lease next time. No hot people. Only quiet people who wore lots of clothes. Maybe an Amish person. That would save on the electric bill, too.

Yes, of course. The only answer to his problem was kicking Lindsey out and getting an Amish neighbor. Why hadn't he thought of that earlier?

Oh, because it's a dumb idea, his inner Myron told him.

Shaking his head, he unlocked the garage, eager to get to work. Or, more likely, eager to stare blankly at a pile of scrap metal and hope inspiration struck.

Looking at the stuff he'd salvaged from the junkyard, he waited. And waited.

It wasn't that he couldn't see what was intrinsically interesting about the shapes and lines of an old muffler, a set of lead pipes, a spider's web of different colored wires. He knew that once he polished up the fender and the hubcaps, they'd look cool. But he wasn't seeing . . . anything beyond the pile of potentially shiny crap in the middle of the garage.

And that's what scared him. Because his gift had always been seeing a pile of crap like a puzzle. And not just like a set of pieces to put together; he could look at the puzzle and see what it would look like finished. It was easy.

Not that welding and smashing and shaping things into the finished product wasn't hard work, but the vision always came easily.

It was all Lindsey's fault.

Ever since she moved in, he had no interest in hard lines and sharp surfaces.

Ever since she moved in, he was obsessed with softness and light.

Dammit. He didn't do softness and light.

He didn't like compromising. He knew it made him sound like a pretentious jerk, but he didn't want anything clouding his vision. He had to see something clearly to be inspired. He could see the tree, see how it had managed to defy nature and grow out of that isolated rock, see the tenacity in that little seed to cling to whatever it could to reach for the sun.

And now the tree was dead. It had reached the sun, and then it had died.

Even though that idea made him want to put on a black turtleneck and smoke French Gauloises cigarettes, that was what he had seen as he stood on the top of the hill. That was what had drawn him to that one tree—the beauty in the tragedy, the embodiment of the truth that everything comes to an end. It had moved him.

But as he stood back and looked at the bones of the stretching branches, he wasn't feeling the same power. It was just . . . a tree. Or, it wasn't a tree. It was a set of welded-together metal rods that vaguely formed the shape of a tree.

He closed his eyes, turned away from the sculpture. He had to shake this off. Everyone had their moments of doubt. He'd had them before: the fear that he would never be able to capture what he saw in the metal.

Was this just the usual self-doubt and anxiety? Could he shake it off? He'd never felt quite so . . . disheartened before.

It was the pressure. There were three artists in this show, as opposed to a dozen. The next step was a solo show, then a show in London, then art fairs. This was big. This was what he wanted, to make his living creating. When he'd finally had enough to buy a house, the duplex had seemed like a great idea—the rental income would get him through lean times.

These were definitely going to be lean times if he didn't get his head out of his butt. Staring at the walls of his studio was not going to help matters. He needed to get his mind off things, come back with a fresh perspective.

He thought of Lindsey, soft and light and wearing shorts and a stethoscope.

No. Bad. He needed the kind of distraction that did not involve creeping on his tenant. He needed the opposite kind of distraction.

He'd visit Myron. An old man in a nursing home who would tell him the exact, specific kind of idiot he was being. The best medicine for what ailed him.

Chapter 7

Lindsey was half-looking over Hope's notes from the night before, but she kept being distracted by the photos on the desk the three nurses shared. Hope had twins, a boy and a girl, who were just starting high school this year, and last year's school pictures stared back at Lindsey.

Before coming to this job, Lindsey had been concerned that her age would be a problem for Hope and Evan. She was younger than both of them, and even though she had valuable experience working in larger nursing homes, they still had more years on her. Plus, she had the cushy shift. Seven AM to three PM—as close to a normal workday as any nurse could ask for.

But Hope liked working the night shift because it paid better and she got home in time to have breakfast with her family and get the kids to school. Evan hated mornings, and going home at eleven gave him plenty of time to get ready for gigs with his horror-punk band. He'd showed her a picture of them online. She still had a hard time reconciling the image of the soft-spoken, chubby Evan with the bloody-eyed zombie drummer. She wondered if she could talk Mary Beth into going to one of the shows with her.

Since the schedule worked out for everyone, Lindsey decided to quit feeling guilty. Besides, she was the boss now. She could only hope that all of her hard decisions would work out so smoothly.

But the photos were distracting her. Not that Lindsey would consider putting a moratorium on personal effects on their shared desk. (Although she, like her predecessor, put the kibosh on Evan's B-Movie Gore calendar. They had enough boobs and blood in their real lives.) The kids were cute. Danielle wore pigtails, glasses and a sullen look— Hope said she was channeling Wednesday Addams. David sported his braces proudly, if his maniacal grin were any indication. He was now apparently also sporting an earring, courtesy of his sister.

They were a handful, Hope was fond of saying. Depending on the day, that was either followed by "and they're worth it" or "I'm going to join the circus because it will be less chaotic."

Lindsey wanted that.

She wanted happy chaos and frustrated time-outs that she could laugh about later. She wanted a partner she could laugh about them with. It was damn distracting, this biological clock. It was at odds with her Declaration of Independence. She wanted to prove herself separate from her parents, but what was the point if she was just going to attach herself to some guy?

Besides, she had tried attachment, and it hadn't made her happy.

Brad was the son of her dad's golf buddy. He was funny and smart and responsible, and took great care of himself. They had a nice time together. He gave excellent foot rubs when she'd started her rotations. He worked hard, but not too hard that he couldn't make time for her. He liked going out to eat. He didn't mind if she bowed out of tailgating with him and his football friends, even though The Other Girlfriends always went. He was close to his family, he was great with his niece and nephews, he owned a house not too far from where her parents lived.

So when they started talking about officially moving in together, he said he wanted to get married first. Which was so nice and romantic, and made Lindsey break out in hives.

Her doctor, also an old family friend, helped her get to the bottom of her medical distress: she wanted out. She'd lived in the same town her whole life. If she married Brad, she would never leave. Admitting that made the hives go away, but it started the anxiety. What was wrong with her? Brad was perfect. Brad was wonderful. Brad would take excellent care of her.

But she wanted to take care of herself. And she wanted to see what else was out there in the world. Not romantically—she would have stayed with Brad if he'd have let her. But just—what are other people like? What makes them tick?

The job in Willow Springs was a great opportunity. It was a step up in her career, the salary was good, the town was adorable, and Kentucky was probably about as different from Arizona as she was going to get. Plus, her certifications were reciprocal. It was as if some divine hand had cleared a path for her and said, "Here, Lindsey, take this road."

There was plenty of time for her to find a guy and make Terror Twins of her own. Even though she was practically thirty—that was the clock talking, not her. Besides, she was barely here long enough to make friends, let alone jump into a potential love match.

And then there was Walker.

Nope. No. Today was the day she promised herself she wouldn't think about Walker Smith and his hot body and his jerky attitude that made her want to taunt him even more.

Although.

If she were putting off finding the Future Mr. Lindsey to focus on taking care of herself... wouldn't Walker be an excellent option? She was definitely attracted to him, and she thought he might be attracted to her. Plus, he was aggressively unpleasant, and he obviously couldn't stand her, so the chances of their developing deeper feelings for each other were, gosh, practically none.

There was no way she would fall for a guy like Walker Smith.

She looked at the clock. Seven thirty-two on a mild Tuesday morning in small-town Kentucky. She should write that down. That was the moment she finally lost her damn mind.

Also, past time to get the day started. She picked up the chart Hope had left behind, happy to see that all of the early risers had already been fed and watered, as Evan liked to say. She would have to check with Janice, the morning care aide, to make sure she actually saw Mrs. Harper swallow her pills. And then Lindsey would say a prayer of thanks that she'd inherited such a competent staff.

She would have to corral some of the kitchen guys to help her set up the sunroom after breakfast. The Bookmobile was coming. Well, a cargo van full of crates of library books was coming. Doug, the librarian, was just a little less new to town than she was, and he'd been coming to read to the residents for a few months now. At first some of them had chafed at the idea of "storytime," but now it was one of the most popular activities.

Anyway, the Bookmobile was much less stress than the "therapy dogs" that Billie Monroe from the vet's office brought in two weeks ago. Sure, the dogs were cute, and the residents loved them, but she was pretty sure the entire staff was going to walk out after the dogs got into the toilet paper and the pantry and . . . well, it wasn't worth rehashing. Billie stayed to clean up and said she would bring fewer puppies next time. Lindsey did not want to deter an enthusiastic volunteer, but she was pretty sure there was not going to be a next time. Maybe therapy cats instead.

Anyway, she could handle the Bookmobile. It would be nice to see Doug again. He was pretty quiet, but she hoped he would come out of his shell enough to hang out. She needed some friends.

Since her neighbor was definitely not one of them.

And there was Walker again, pushing his way into her consciousness. It wasn't fair. He didn't spend all of his time pining over her friendship; why should she?

Enough Walker, she told herself for the sixty thousandth time, and grabbed up her chart to start morning rounds.

Myron was not a morning person, which was one thing he and Walker had in common. And unlike Walker's current neighbor, Myron wouldn't have dreamed of an early morning booty shake.

And no amount of coffee would have prepared Walker for that image. He had a feeling no amount of whiskey would erase it.

Even though it was early for lunch, Walker knew it was just the right time to see Myron. He would have had enough breakfast to take his mind off the fact that he was no longer allowed to drink caffeine, but he would have spent enough time in the breakfast room to get into an argument with someone, so he'd be ready to go.

Walker had it all figured out. He'd take Myron to that little family restaurant in Hollow Bend, they'd do a lap around the Duck Puddle, then they'd hit the theater in the student building at Pembroke. Myron used to teach the woman who managed it now, and she always let them in for film class screenings, even though, clearly, they were not students.

But apparently the day had decided it was not done messing with him. Walker squeezed his truck in to the last remaining spot beside the library van, which annoyed him. Did it have to take up so many spaces? It also reminded him that he had an overdue book in his living room, which also annoyed him. He tried to shake off the feeling as he entered the carefully regulated temperature of the nursing home, but he needn't have bothered schooling his features for his friend's benefit. Myron wasn't paying attention to him. Instead, Myron stood in the center of a circle of chairs, about to come to blows with Eugene May.

Walker stood back, assessing the situation. Myron's face was definitely red, which Walker didn't like. Eugene was so worked up, he seemed to be spitting more than shouting. A bearded guy in a green dress shirt was trying to get between them. As Walker moved closer, he heard the guy saying something about there being plenty of time for *two* stories and he would be glad to leave the books here.

Walker knew that the only thing Myron liked less than being wrong was Eugene May, who had apparently stolen Myron's senior prom date and married her. Even after Myron married the love of his life, he still would not forgive Eugene. Walker knew this because he had heard the story of this particular indignity every day since Myron moved into the home and found his archrival living down the hall.

Eugene seemed all right to Walker. He wore his pants a little high, but he loved his grandkids and talked to Walker about fishing. He didn't want to be disloyal to Myron, though. But when Myron lifted a heavy bestseller over his head, Walker had to side with Eugene. And Eugene's head.

He reached Myron and grabbed his wrist just as a voice shouted behind him, "Mr. Harris!"

Myron, Eugene, Walker, and the guy all turned at once toward the shouter.

The woman of his nightmares stood before him, wearing bright pink scrubs and spotless white shoes.

Of course. Mother Teresa.

Walker had just about forgotten that she worked at Shady Grove, which was much better than admitting that he came to see Myron in the hopes of accidentally running into Lindsey. That was crazy.

Walker saw the moment Lindsey recognized him, but to her credit, she quickly shook off the confusion and headed into the fray. Not that the fracas was much of one anymore, what with her school marm-ing them into submission.

"What's going on here?" she demanded, pulling the book from Myron's hand. Walker dropped his wrist and took a step back.

"Jesse Stuart is an American treasure!" Eugene shouted.

"You made Doug read Jesse Stuart last week," Myron shouted back. "And the week before that!"

"Jesse Stuart is a Kentucky treasure!" Eugene shouted, emphasis on the Kentucky. "All you want to read are those Yankee writers! Or worse, a writer who's not even American!"

"Jesus, Eugene, the Civil War ended a hundred and fifty years ago. Get over it." Myron turned to Lindsey. "Wouldn't you rather hear something different?" Myron turned to Doug. "Wouldn't you rather read something new?" Myron turned to the rows of chairs and stretched his arms out. "Isn't it time for a change?"

The assembled seniors clapped politely. Walker rolled his eyes.

"Mr. Harris, I understand your frustration, but this is not the way we handle conflict." Lindsey handed the book back to Doug, who wisely tucked it into a nearby crate.

"How about Flannery O'Connor?" Doug suggested, holding up a tattered yellow paperback. "We haven't read her yet," he said to Myron, "and she's Southern," he said to Eugene.

"Southern ain't the same as Appalachian," muttered Eugene.

"Oh, sit down and let the man read," a woman called out from the front row.

"Thank you, Mrs. Mitchell," said Lindsey. "Mr. Harris, Mr. May, do you have anything you want to say before we all take our seats?"

The two men mumbled under their breath. Walker didn't think either sounded very sorry.

"Oh, they don't have to apologize on our account," said Mrs. Mitchell. "It's nice to see the old boys still have some spark left in 'em." The other women laughed.

"That's one word for it," muttered Lindsey as everyone settled into a chair. "Doug? They're all yours."

He thanked her, looking a little dubious, and started to read.

Forgetting all about the reason he'd come in—to spring Myron for lunch—Walker tried to back out of the room before anyone really noticed him. He was just about through the doorway, when suddenly Mother Teresa was in front of him.

"Can I help you with something?" she said in a voice that sounded like a candy bar with razor blade filling.

"No, uh—" He gestured lamely to Myron, then the door, then shook his head at his own genius.

She waited, not quite patiently, for him to pull his head out of his ass.

"Myron," he finally spat out. "I came to take Myron to lunch."

Lindsey peered around him at Doug's rapt audience. "He doesn't look available. Myron never misses the Bookmobile."

"I know that."

"Next time maybe you should call ahead to see if he's available."

"I was going to surprise him."

"Well, I could have told you he would be otherwise occupied."

"Well, I didn't know you worked here," he lied. Because it was definitely mature to up the snottiness by matching her increasingly snotty tone.

She took a deep breath, and Walker was seventy-six percent sure he saw her roll her eyes. "How do you know Mr. Harris? Is he family?"

"No, he's . . ." He was family. Just not biological family. But Myron was an adult, and he wasn't a prisoner. He could have friends who took him to lunch. Why couldn't Walker be that friend?

"You're not on the list of his family. That's why I ask."

"So I'm not allowed to visit?"

"No, but Mr. Harris is my responsibility. I don't want to let just anyone take him out of here."

"Just anyone? What do you think, I'm gonna kidnap him? That smartass old know-it-all?"

Lindsey raised her eyebrow at him.

Walker ran his hand over his face. This was going all wrong. "Look. Myron is a friend. Sometimes I take him to lunch. I don't always tell him beforehand. Obviously he's busy today. I'll come back another time."

Lindsey's expression softened. Walker didn't want it to soften. "He really looks forward to the Bookmobile."

"Why do you keep calling it the Bookmobile? It's not even a Bookmobile! It's a van with books that takes up too many parking spaces!"

Lindsey put a hand on his arm. He flinched. "I'm sorry, Walker. I don't think he even noticed you're here."

Walker looked over to where Myron sat with the others, in rapt attention as the librarian read. Knowing Myron and his love for stories, Walker had to agree that, no, Myron probably hadn't seen him.

"But you're welcome to stay," Lindsey said. "Doug will read another twenty minutes, then they all check out books and talk his ear off. We serve lunch right afterward. You can see if Myron wants to go out then. Although I should warn you, the lunch after the Bookmobile is when Myron and Eugene do their best literary debating."

"They don't just clobber each other with books?"

She laughed. She laughed and Walker wished he hadn't made that stupid joke because she looked beautiful when she laughed.

He was losing his damn mind.

"I should go," he said, but then he heard a "psst" and Myron was gesturing him over. So Walker pulled up a chair at the back of the group and sat and listened to the bearded man in the green dress shirt read a story.

Chapter 8

Walker didn't stay for lunch. Lindsey tried to pretend she wasn't disappointed, but she was no good at lying to herself. It was just that Walker seemed so different around Myron. Sure, he scowled and moped and it didn't look like he said much—although even she had trouble getting a word in edgewise with Myron. But he also smiled and laughed a little. As he was leaving, Myron shook his hand and pulled him in for a hug, whispering something in his ear and giving him a gruff kiss on the cheek.

Apparently Walker was capable of behaving in a way that encouraged warm feelings in others, after all.

And Lindsey's Curiosity Radar went into overdrive.

Detective Lindsey was not a side of her personality that she was especially proud of. Not ashamed, exactly, but Detective Lindsey had gotten her into more trouble than she cared for. For example, finding out her sixth grade teacher's orthopedic shoes did not hide a prosthetic leg after all. Or that her prom date was not a cross-dresser; he was just carrying around another girl's underwear.

"How is your lunch, Mr. Harris?" she asked, just as she would have asked any other resident. No big deal.

Myron ran his fork through a white blob on his plate. "These aren't real mashed potatoes, are they?"

Lindsey knew they were mashed cauliflower, because even though the residents were full-grown adults, some guys just didn't want to eat their vegetables. Besides, she had tasted them before they came out of the kitchen. They were pretty good.

Slathered in butter, they weren't bad.

Better than dessert, anyway. But she had never been a real big fan of Jell-O with fruit cocktail in it.

Lindsey rearranged the napkins on the table. "I saw your friend Walker was here."

"Shame he couldn't stay for lunch." Myron picked up a forkful of "potato," let it fall back on his plate. It *plopped*.

"Yes, but at least he got to see you get into a cat fight with Mr. May."

"Call me Eugene!" Eugene yelled from his table across the room.

"He started it!" Myron pushed his plate away, pulled his Jell-O closer.

"I'm pretty sure you were the one threatening him with a book, Mr. Harris."

"Call me Myron. And that wasn't a book. That was a mystery with cats in it."

"Hey, what's wrong with a cat mystery?" Gladys asked from across the table.

"Have you ever met a cat? If a human was killed, the cat wouldn't give a crap. The cat would just sit on the furniture and stare at the dead body until someone else came in to feed it."

"Mr. Harris—Myron—be nice. Remember what Doug said?"

"Never judge another person's reading taste. Which is bullshit. Pardon the language."

"Well, the whole thing made you miss a lunch date with your . . ." She waved her hand, waiting for Myron to fill in the blank. "With your Walker." She cringed.

Myron sighed and looked a little guilty. "He's good to me, that boy."

"You really look forward to the Bookmobile, so I was just surprised to see your . . . Walker visiting."

"Yeah, he takes me out to lunch and walks me. It's the least he can do after he ratted me out to my daughter."

"Ratted you out? What did you do?"

"I fell a few times. So what? Nobody ever died from falling a few times."

That wasn't true, but Lindsey wisely kept her mouth shut. She knew Myron's health condition. He'd had a series of mini-strokes that left little damage, in the grand scheme of things, but nonetheless prevented him from living completely independently. He'd lost some mobility on his left side, leaving him with a small limp and a hand that could not grip. Stairs were pretty much impossible unaided.

And he was forgetful. Not about big things, like people's names and the relative merits of the major American writers of the twentieth century. But his bluster had made it hard to spot that he was constantly leaving the stove on, forgetting to shower. He was vulnerable, and he was just unwell enough to be dangerous.

He also refused to leave Willow Springs. That was why his daughter moved him to Shady Grove.

Lindsey hadn't met his daughter, Darlene, yet, but she'd spoken to her on the phone. She was quiet and sounded very sweet, and expressed mucho gratitude for the care Myron was receiving. And she expressed mucho mucho guilt that she couldn't get down to see him more than once a month, if that. But she lived on a small farm and it was over two hours away when the roads were good, which they often were not, and she had three boys and . . . Lindsey had heard many excuses from family members about why they could not visit their parents once they put them in a home. But as she spoke to Darlene, Lindsey found it difficult to maintain the hardened heart with which she usually listened to these excuses. She knew that Darlene called her father every morning once the kids left for school, and every night after dinner. She saw in the guest book that Darlene did in fact come down almost once a month. But Myron had insisted on Shady Grove, and Darlene knew he would be well taken care of.

By Walker.

Lindsey gave her head a mental slap. Of course. The neighbor. The duplex with the stairs. Walker ratted him out . . . because Myron lived next door to him. Myron was the gardener. Myron was the guy who'd lived in her apartment before.

Small world.

Small town.

So, if Myron used to live next door to Walker . . . No, she shouldn't grill a poor old man just to get information.

"How long have you known Walker?"

Myron shrugged. "Since he was a kid."

To Myron, everyone under the age of sixty was a kid. "That's a long time."

"Eh, I lost track of him after he moved away with his no-good father. But he came back to town and bought the house I was living in, and he didn't kick me out so he could . . . what's that called? Toss it?"

"Flip it?"

"Yeah. He didn't toss me out just so he could flip it. There's another guy in town who does that. But not Walker."

"Walker seems . . . nice," Lindsey gently finished.

Myron laughed. "He ain't a junkyard dog, but only barely. But he's a good kid. He takes good care of me." He cleared his throat.

"Well, he seems to like you. So he's clearly insane."

Myron smiled. "Nah, he ain't got a real family so he has to put up with me."

Lindsey's beeper went off. Mae Mitchell needed her afternoon meds. Lindsey paused, then quickly unpaused in horror. No matter how good the gossip was suddenly getting, digging up dirt on her landlord, who apparently was capable of human emotion after all, was not more important than making sure people's blood sugar was okay. *Even though it's getting good,* she thought, as she hurried over to Mae.

He sniffed along the side of the road. The road itself actually smelled really good, but last time he explored that, he almost got run over. Not fun. And he already knew that those cars were much faster than he was, although sometimes he still liked to try to catch one.

Still, next to the road there was plenty of grass, and a while back, he smelled a deer. He never smelled deer in the yard, not since the old guy planted all that stinky green stuff.

But he wasn't just here to smell the deer, even though he sort of lost track of his mission every time he picked up the scent. No. No matter how good the deer smelled, it was more important that he find out where those two were going every day, and to make sure they really came back.

Sometimes they'd go in separate directions, which made it tough. He could never decide which one to follow, and he would get so tired running around in circles that he would just go to sleep under the porch. But today he decided to follow the lady. And then—the guy showed up! Maybe they were going to the same place after all!

Which meant they would come home together. Which meant he had to hurry. He didn't know why he had to hurry, but suddenly he just felt like he had to RUN.

Chapter 9

Two days.

It was two days since she'd seen Walker. She'd knocked on his door after work the night after the Bookmobile. Just for a friendly chat about his old pal, Myron. And also to apologize for misjudging him. He might be an abrasive jerk, but he was also apparently quite kind.

She was still working on the apology part.

It didn't matter. He hadn't answered, and rather than make herself look (more) desperate, she called Mary Beth to see if she wanted to hang out. But Mary Beth's baby was sick, so Lindsey called Billie the dog wrangler. But Billie's boyfriend was sick, so she promised a rain check. So Lindsey stayed home and talked to her mom and watched TV and pretended not to look out her kitchen window at the garage. She was feeling lonely and annoyed that the only two people she knew were not available. Then she was annoyed at herself for being annoyed at them, because it wasn't their fault that they all had someone to take care of and Lindsey was home alone in sweatpants after taking care of people for a living all day.

If only she had someone to take care of.

Nope. No. No one to take care of but herself. That was what she wanted. So she took a bath, took care of herself, and felt a little better about life in the morning.

These things just take time, her mom had warned her in an uncharacteristic show of support. So the next day after work, when Billie called to say that Andrew, the boyfriend, was still sick but driving her crazy, Lindsey took her up on the offer of a movie. And when, this morning, Mary Beth called to apologize for not being able to hang out earlier, but the baby was all better now, Lindsey got an idea.

The idea had nothing at all to do with Walker, which made her feel very proud. However, it also involved discussing a little with him beforehand, which also made her feel very proud.

After a morning of kneeling in her mess of a garden, Lindsey got her chance. She hopped out of what-some-would-call-a-garden to stop Walker on his way to the garage.

"Hey!"

He stopped short. He looked a little like a deer in headlights, which Lindsey could verify, having almost hit her first deer on the way home from the movies the night before.

She tried again. "Hi."

Now he looked like a puzzled deer in headlights.

"Listen, I'm going to have a few people over tonight. Is that okay?"

"Why wouldn't it be?"

"I don't know. I thought maybe you might have to . . . work . . . late." She lamely indicated the garage.

He gave her a puzzled look.

"Here in the garage. Where you work."

He didn't say anything at first, and Lindsey hoped that he was gearing up to give her a lengthy and satisfying explanation about why his art needed to be a solitary endeavor and that, in fact, he was not making meth.

Finally, he spoke. "It's fine."

She tried not to let her disappointment show. "We won't make too much noise."

"Okay."

"It's just a few people. You're welcome to stop by," she added, hopefully. But not too hopefully. She didn't want to scare him off. With normal human hospitality.

He just looked at her, and she held his eyes, trying to decipher the look. Was he flattered? Was he pleased? Was he horrified that she would invite him over to a girls' night wine and cheese party?

"No, thanks. I have to work."

And he headed into the garage.

She blew her bangs out of her eyes. She would never make it as a detective. She would have to distract herself with unpacking her wine glasses.

* * *

Walker picked up a mallet. Now she was going to have a girls' night? That wasn't quiet at all. That was why he missed Myron. Myron never had girls' nights where women came over and . . . Walker didn't actually know what happened on a girls' night. He had seen a bachelorette party at a bar once. Walker didn't really hang out at the kind of bars that would be appealing to people in furry tiaras. But they made themselves at home anyway, and Walker left that night with his ears ringing and his wallet lighter. They shrieked a lot. And he might have been cajoled into buying a few rounds.

He thought that would shut them up.

Also, they were pretty.

He didn't know why Lindsey's girls' night bothered him so much. It had nothing to do with him, as he'd so eloquently told her. His exciting Saturday night plans included staying in the garage, hammering pieces of scrap metal into shapes. He might even drink a beer while he worked.

So what if he didn't need to socialize? He was a lone wolf. He didn't need a pack—his dad had taught him that. He howled once, hammered the metal twice.

"There's only one thing you can count on in this world, kid," Red Smith was fond of saying. "And that's that people will always let you down." He spent Walker's entire childhood proving himself right. The best present Red ever gave his son was getting indicted for fraud two weeks after Walker's eighteenth birthday. Ten years in federal prison, and it was all the other guy's fault. The judge had it in for him. The guy who bought his work shouldn't have been such a rube. It didn't matter. Walker hadn't seen Red in over ten years, and he was okay with that. He sent a letter every year on Red's birthday—only because Myron insisted—but that was it. Never got a reply. Never wanted one.

What did Pollyanna know about what he wanted? Nothing. She didn't know anything about him. He didn't need anyone. He heard noises coming from the open windows in her apartment. So he cranked up the music and pounded the hell out of some scrap metal.

Lindsey held the door open and tried not to squeal with glee. Mary Beth inched past her with a tower of pastries baked by her stepfather. She was followed up the stairs by Billie from the vet's office and her best friend, Katie. They were getting settled in when the doorbell rang, and Grace, who was engaged to Mary Beth's brother, and Helen, a librarian who worked with Grace at Pembroke College, came in bearing wine.

Grace held up a bottle in each hand. "Semester's over, baby!"

"Sorry this isn't a more exciting way to kick off your summer break," Lindsey said.

"No, this is perfect—Jake didn't have to pretend he was okay missing poker night to celebrate with me," Grace explained.

"So we're the next best thing?" Mary Beth teased.

"He would have stayed home and you know it," Helen said, nudging Grace with her hip.

"Yeah, but then he wouldn't owe me any favors when I get home tonight."

Everyone laughed, except for Mary Beth, who grimaced at the thought of her brother and favors. But she grimaced with love, Lindsey thought.

She was still nervous, though. She really wanted MB and Billie and their friends to like her, and she wanted to like them. Lindsey had met plenty of friendly people here in Willow Springs, but that wasn't the same as making friends. She needed friends. She was a social person. And she had never lived anywhere where she didn't know anyone.

And now here she was, in a kitchen full of food with potential friends and, thanks to her own shopping spree and Grace and Helen's contribution, more wine than six women should probably consume.

But gosh darn it, they would try.

"Nice spread," Grace said, dipping a piece of bread into the spinach-artichoke dip. "Oh my god!" she said around her mouthful. "Amazing spread."

"Thanks," Lindsey said, digging the corkscrew out of the drawer. "It's my mom's recipe. I was going to make her salsa, but I couldn't find the right kind of peppers."

"Right, you're from Arizona. Whole different set of food out there, I bet," said Mary Beth.

Lindsey shrugged, not wanting to make a big deal. But she did miss the food. They had a Mexican restaurant in Willow Springs, but it was nothing like what she was used to. And the grocery store had all of the basics, but no exotic surprises. Well, except for the pawpaw jam she bought from the Women's Club van parked outside the grocery store. It tasted like mango and banana and was apparently native to the region. She'd looked it up online, and the leaves looked sort of like something growing on the nursing home grounds, but definitely not something she had ever seen before.

Anyway, she thought she could grow some of what she wanted in the garden out back, but she was also going to have to accept that not everything in Kentucky was going to be the same as what she was used to.

Which was the point, right?

Boo.

It was a perfect night, so they forewent the Girl Movie selection and pulled every chair she owned onto the porch. Mary Beth joined them after stopping to call home, her cheeks flushed from just half a glass of wine. "Sorry, I just had to check up on Will."

"How's he doing with my perfect cousin, Cody?" Katie asked.

"Oh, he's fine. Will's got the baby thing down. Bottles, blankies, all that stuff."

"But?" Lindsey prompted.

"I just hate to leave him! I already moved my office into our spare bedroom, but I feel guilty every time I leave to show a house. This is the first time I've been out socially all month. I feel like I should be home with them! No offense, Lindsey."

"Oh." Lindsey started to feel her own guilt for pulling MB away from her family.

"But as Will rightly pointed out," said Grace, refilling MB's wine glass, "you need to take a break. And there'll be plenty of diapers to change tomorrow and he *will* save the really poopy ones for you."

"I don't remember him saying that," MB said, sipping her wine.

"Maybe Jake said that," Grace conceded.

"Hmm. That sounds like something a little brother would say."

Lindsey just smiled as the two women bantered. She'd met Will once, and had heard a lot about Jake from Grace and MB, but didn't really know them well enough to know why their comments were funny. She didn't even have any siblings of her own, so how would she know what a little brother would say? She felt the strange sensation of watching the whole conversation from the outside of the fish bowl.

Probably just the wine talking already.

"Anyway, Will said Jake would pick us up when he's done with poker night. That's not too late, is it?" MB asked Lindsey.

"No, it's fine. Stay as long as you want."

"Thanks. So—" Grace turned to Lindsey. "How about you? Have you got a man to annoy you?" MB shoved her shoulder lightly.

"No," Lindsey laughed. "No one to annoy me but myself."

"This is a cute house. You lucked out," said Billie. "It seems to be in great shape."

"Yeah, I guess Walker takes good care of it."

"So, no random doors falling off or towel rods collapsing?" asked Grace.

"No!" said Lindsey, shocked. "Has that happened here before?"

"It happened to Grace," said MB.

"Yeah, right after she sold me the house," said Grace.

"Hey, Jake helped you out!" Mary Beth obviously thought her brother's handyman skills compensated for any lack in the house itself.

"Yeah," said Grace, her face going a little dreamy. "Yeah, he did."

"And now it's in perfect shape," Katie said with a shrug.

Grace snorted. "Now the plaster in the bedroom is cracking. It's Jake's fault. He keeps tinkering. I tell him to just leave well enough alone, but he can't help himself."

"The joys of cohabitation," said MB.

"Consider yourself lucky, Lindsey," said Billie. "God, that sounded really annoying. I used to hate it when people in a couple would tell me how good I had it as a single person."

Lindsey laughed. That was one of her least favorite things in the world. What was wrong with wanting her own space? What was wrong with not wanting to be Mrs. Brad?

"Trust me, I know. You think any man would put up with that blue velvet couch in there?" Katie pointed through the open screen door. "No offense."

"None taken. I love it. I can't help it if that tacky couch speaks to me. Although apparently I'm the only one."

"No . . . it's great."

Lindsey laughed again. "It's fine! You don't have to like it. You don't have to live with it, right?"

Katie raised her glass and took a drink.

"Anyway, your reaction is nowhere near as bad as Walker's."

"What do you mean?" asked Helen, and suddenly all ten eyes

were on Lindsey. Apparently she wasn't the only one starved for information on Walker Smith.

"Well, he saw it when it was delivered, and it was pretty clear that he was not impressed."

"Wait, Walker made a facial expression?" Grace asked. "That's a first."

"You know him?" Lindsey asked, knowing perfectly well that she did. MB had told her. It was one of the reasons she'd wanted to try to befriend Grace. And because she had no other friends. Because she was obviously a terrible person.

"Sure. The gallery at Pembroke included his work in an exhibit of regional artists last year. He came to the exhibit, but I don't think he said two words. Wait, I heard him tell the president, 'Thanks.' That was about it."

"That's one word," said Katie.

"His friend talked enough for him," said MB. "That's what Jake told me."

"That guy was pretty great," Helen said. "He really knew his art. For a while I had a bet going with one of the art professors that Myron was really the artist, and Walker was just some kind of hot, grumpy front for the operation."

Myron. So Myron went with Walker to art openings? And talked for him? Knowing Myron, that was no surprise.

"Why would they do that?" asked Billie.

"I don't know, to cultivate some mystery? You have to admit, Walker Smith gets people talking."

Billie shrugged. Lindsey wanted to shake her. *What do you know about Walker that has you not talking?*

"Oh, do you know him well?" Lindsey asked over her wine glass, totally nonchalant and not at all clinging to her composure by her fingernails.

"Nope," said Billie. "Too old for me. But I think he went to high school with Jake, right?"

"For a little while, but Jake barely knows him," said Grace. "I asked. I mean, how can you go to a school as small as Willow Springs High and not know a guy in your class?"

"I guess he was in and out of school a lot. I know his dad moved around. For work, I think. Although I'm not really sure what he did.

All I know is that Walker came back here a few years ago, bought this house, and he's been renting out this half ever since."

"And mysteriously making art in his secret garage lair," Lindsey said, then took a dramatic gulp of wine.

"That's his studio?" Helen asked. "What's he working on?"

"I have no idea. He sure doesn't talk to me about it, but then, he doesn't talk to me about anything. Or, really, talk at all. Anyway, I'm not allowed in the garage. And he keeps it locked."

Everyone took a disappointed sip of wine.

"Oh my gosh, you tried to break in," Katie said suddenly.

"What kind of tenant are you?" Mary Beth shouted, sloshing a little wine onto her lap. "Breaking and entering!"

"Hey, it was only attempted breaking and entering!" She explained to them about the couch, and the boxers, and her attempts to apologize that culminated in her peeking into the garage, and, when she couldn't see in, trying the door handle. Just so she could apologize! Not at all so she could catch a glimpse of his art and, if the stars were aligned, his naked back!

MB snorted her wine, and they all dissolved into shrieks of laughter.

He wanted to follow the big one into the garage, but the lady was still out there, watching. She'd been digging around in his garden again. He didn't understand what she was doing. She was digging, but she wasn't eating anything. She would just pull up some plants (the ones that tasted the worst, so he was grateful), then put them in a pile. Then, when he wasn't looking, the pile would disappear. That was probably good, because even though those plants did not agree with his belly, they smelled really good and they were all there in a pile and it was very difficult for him to avoid sticking his whole head into the pile and eating his way out. That would be so much fun. Maybe she would make a pile of the good stuff. Or he could make a pile of the good stuff.

By the time he had his pile of good stuff planned out, the man was gone, behind that locked door again. And the lady was gone, too. He could start his pile now. Or, he could see where that rabbit was going. Or that squirrel. What were all these creatures doing in his yard? This was going to call for some stealth . . .

* * *

They were never going to leave. Walker was never going to be able to use his front porch again. His front porch or the front door. All because Mother Teresa was never going to kick out the gaggle of women playing *Sex and the City* on her porch. Wine. Who drank wine in Kentucky?

Fine, so a lot of other people drank wine around here. But he still didn't like it. He didn't like that they were making so much noise on his porch. Or at least right next to his porch. What if he wanted to sleep? Fine, so it was barely ten o'clock on a Saturday night, and he had already established with Lindsey that he had pretty weird sleep patterns, so she probably wasn't torturing him on purpose.

Mostly he was just mad because he suspected that Mother Teresa was out there with that million-dollar smile and he was inside the garage, making a stupid metal tree that reflected the beauty and tragedy of nature.

He was jealous that she was making friends.

Because, what? He wanted her to himself?

No, because if she made friends, then she would make more noise and he would never sleep again.

Disgusted, he disentangled himself from the sheets and threw on his old jeans. If he wasn't going to sleep, he was going to work. And by work, he meant stare at a big honking pile of metal in his garage.

As he stalked out to the garage, he heard a *yip* and a rustle in the side yard. He paused, but there was nothing else. Just his heavy breathing and more laughter carrying over from the front porch of the house. He unlocked the garage and shut the door behind him. Despite the open space inside, he felt closed in. Fine. He would keep the door open, even if that meant hearing shouts and laughter. He swore he could hear them pouring more wine out there.

Well, if they were going to keep him up, he was going to keep them up. He scrolled around on his phone until he found a playlist that was both angry and nostalgic, then plugged it into the dock on the shelf over his workbench. He set the list to shuffle, and gave a small inner headbang as the intro guitar wailed. Then he got to work.

Walker didn't know how much time had passed, and he was barely aware of how much progress he'd made, when he was interrupted by a banging on the garage door. He instinctively looked toward the door that was open to the yard—nobody there. But something was definitely banging. He looked at the time on his phone—two AM. Who could that be at this hour?

Armed with a ballpeen hammer and a small tube of industrial-strength epoxy, he pushed the button on the garage door opener and stepped back. As the door slowly creaked and squeaked its way up, Walker was faced with black boots, jeans, a holstered weapon, and, eventually, a really pissed off looking Chief Will Brakefield.

Walker saw Brakefield's arm go for his hip, so he put the hammer down. Then the glue. Hands up, he asked, "Can I help you?" Brakefield pointed to his ears.

"What?" Walker shouted.

"Music," Brakefield shouted back.

Oh. Walker moved quickly to the workbench and turned it off. The sudden quiet felt oddly heavy, until it was broken by the barking of neighborhood dogs.

Walker turned back to Chief Brakefield, who was stepping into the garage.

"I got a few calls about the noise," he said.

"Oh," said Walker, thinking about Lindsey and her laughing fun party. She couldn't just come knock on the garage and ask him to shut up? She had to call the police?

"This isn't the first time I've had a call about you making a racket all night," Brakefield continued. "But it's been a while."

Back before Myron took him in hand, Walker used to lose track of the noise he made when he was lost in a project. But when he was conscious of an old man across the yard, he learned to work in a more tenant-friendly environment. Also, he bought headphones.

He forgot about the other neighbors.

Walker usually tried to be as unobtrusive as possible. His preferred state of existence was for no one to know he was there. That sometimes conflicted with his need for an occasional metal-fest (musical and otherwise). But he truly had not been aware how loud the music sounded outside, or how late-into-the-night turned into early-in-the-morning.

So much for flying under the radar.

He could try to spin it so this was Lindsey's fault—she'd called the cops, so she was the one bringing attention down on him. And he wouldn't have been blasting hair metal if she hadn't been having such loud fun.

Because of course Red Smith's son would be completely blameless.

Man, that tasted bitter.

"Hey, man, you okay?"

Walker had totally forgotten about Chief Brakefield, standing there while he gave his conscience a workout.

"Sure," Walker responded curtly.

"You're working pretty late."

"Couldn't sleep."

"Hmm. Not on a deadline or anything?"

Walker shook his head, suddenly aware that someone was in his garage with his unfinished artwork. Chief Brakefield had always been decent to him, but it still made him nervous.

"You take anything to help you stay up?"

Walker wrinkled his forehead in confusion. He didn't take anything except for an unhealthy interest in his neighbor.

Why would he take something to help him stay up? Wasn't that counterproductive for someone with insomnia?

Ah, he thought, suddenly realizing that Chief Brakefield was a cop who would probably be interested if someone was doing something illegal. Like, for example, drugs.

Fortunately, Walker's artistic madness came to him stone cold sober.

"No," he said, looking right at Brakefield. "I don't need drugs to stay up." He had his own crazy head to help him with that.

Brakefield looked at him for a minute, then, apparently satisfied with his sobriety, nodded. "Keep the noise down, will you? I don't like to leave my wife and child in the middle of the night unless it's an actual emergency. I don't need you giving Mrs. Stringer an excuse to call and complain."

"Oh." So it wasn't Lindsey. It was Mrs. Stringer, known busybody and world champion complainer. "Okay."

"Thanks. And . . . Iron Maiden? Seriously?" Without waiting for Walker to explain himself, Chief Brakefield got into his car and drove away.

Walker watched the reflection of the taillights move along the fences down the street, then he flipped the garage door opener and turned back to his work. Suddenly his eyes stung and he realized he was exhausted. As soon as he thought it, his limbs felt like they weighed a ton. He considered just curling up at the base of his tree, but a concrete floor and metal shavings were not very appealing when he had a king-sized pillow top waiting for him inside. There was nothing for it but to drag himself through the yard and into the house.

He had his hand on the doorknob when Lindsey's door opened. She put one foot out onto the back porch. It was far enough to see that she was wearing a tank top and shorts, and her hair was performing amazing, gravity-defying feats.

"Are you okay?" she asked, her voice groggy. "I saw the lights."

Great. Not only had he not succeeded in keeping her up with his loud music, but he had also set himself up as a potential felon.

"It's fine," he said.

"Were you out there working?" she asked through a yawn.

He nodded.

"Do you only work with music in the middle of the night?" She smiled, pleased with her teasing.

"Only when I need to drown out the noise on my own damn front porch." When he saw Lindsey's startled expression, he almost took it back.

"Oh. Okay. Good night." He heard her call as he let the screen door slam behind him.

That was close. He liked people, he really did. But last time he got caught, it didn't turn out so great. He shook his whole body, then did a lap around the fence to remind himself that he wasn't stuck in a cage anymore. That he was free!

And that he was hungry. There was a lot that smelled really good in the yard, but there was one spot where it smelled the best. And that was the spot where the ground was nice and soft and was just begging for his attention. But he'd better do it fast, before the people came out again.

He had a lot of work to do.

Chapter 10

Wine. That was Lindsey's first thought when she woke up. The next was that the sun was way too bright. She had gone to bed without closing the blinds, and her gauzy curtains were doing nothing to keep the room dark. She wanted it dark. She was off today, and she wanted to stay in a cocoon until next spring.

But when she sat up, she realized that her headache was really not so bad. And if she just wore her sunglasses around the house for a little bit, she was sure she'd get back to normal.

That was her professional opinion, anyway.

That and aspirin. And a soda.

And probably a greasy egg sandwich from the diner. It was obviously a nice day. She should walk.

Ugh, exercise.

First, aspirin, then coffee. Too early for soda. Then shower. Then, instead of walking, she could drive to the diner and afterward burn the greasy egg sandwich calories in the garden. She had great plans for the tomato vines, and there were still so many weeds that she was pretty sure pulling them would count as squats.

She settled for coffee and a shower, and then, on account of the nice day, some time in the garden. She couldn't wait for the summer, when she could just step outside and pick herself some dinner. Tomatoes, zucchini, eggplant—the possibilities had her throwing on some shorts and heading out the back door.

But when she got there, she nearly dropped her coffee mug.

Her garden.

Her garden had been completely destroyed.

She had never seen so many roots in her life, probably because she was getting used to them being underground. And her vegetables.

They had only just started growing, but they were large enough for her to recognize the remnants of a zucchini plant, a chewed-up squash blossom, her Little Eggplant That Could, torn up into little pieces. And her tomatoes! It was bad enough that the fruit was ripped from the plants, but the plants were torn out of the ground, too.

How had this happened? Who would do such a thing?

Then she thought of the police lights and the loud music and the grumpy guy next door. But he was just grumpy, not mean. Surely he wouldn't . . .

Maybe he would. He had been pretty upset about last night. But he didn't seem to need quiet, and hadn't asked her to keep it down.

Maybe he didn't want her quiet. Maybe he wanted her gone.

If he wanted to get rid of her, he would have to do a lot more than pull up her garden. The garden that she had pinned so many hopes and dreams on. He probably wouldn't have to do too much more, she thought with a sigh. She was pretty devastated.

She could cry, or she could get revenge.

As she took a slow turn around the yard, she stopped at the door to the garage, and noticed it was open a crack.

She chose revenge.

She pushed the door open, her anger mixing with guilt and fear and anticipation. She really, really didn't want to be surprised with a meth lab. But Walker didn't have that desperate, starving meth look. And he had all of his teeth.

If those were his real teeth.

Shaking her head, she felt along the wall for a light switch. She flicked it up. And her heart stopped.

Because of the windows, she had assumed there was an empty apartment above the garage, but there was no second floor. The high, high ceiling and the concrete floor gave the space the look of a warehouse. There was a small space heater in the corner, and Lindsey thought there was no way that could warm the place in the winter. She imagined Walker in here, blowing on his hands, determined to get back to work.

In the middle of the cold, concrete floor, there was a tree.

It was tall. Lindsey thought it was twice as tall as she was, but that wasn't saying much. She stepped closer so she was standing near the trunk, under some of the branches. Most of the tree looked like it was just a frame, metal pipes welded together to give them shape. But at the bottom, tiny squares of metal were covering the roots and moving up the trunk. Would the whole tree be covered? She looked up through the branches and squinted into the overhead light. It was amazing. Cold and hard and beautiful.

"What are you doing?"

Lindsey spun around, guilt immediately heating her face. Walker stood in the doorway, his hand on the light switch, or maybe he was reaching for one of the metal bars leaning against the wall. She must have woken him up. His hair was a disheveled mess and his boots were untied, but he had managed to throw on his uniform of jeans and ratty T-shirt.

"I didn't touch anything," she said, throwing up her hands.

He didn't look mad, exactly. But he didn't look pleased.

"I'm sorry, I—I wanted to make sure you weren't cooking meth."

He cocked his eyebrow at her.

"Meth is very dangerous," she pointed out.

He shook his head. "I'm not cooking meth."

"No, I see that," she said, turning toward the tree. She had so many questions for him. How much of this did he plan before he started welding? How did he capture that look of bark with something so completely un-bark-y? How did he make something so . . . moving?

But her brain jumbled the questions, and she was a little intimidated by his skill, and maybe a little embarrassed that she had underestimated him. The only question she could get out was, "How will you get this out of here?"

"It comes apart," he said. "And then I'll solder the pieces back together when I install it."

"Walker, it's . . . I had no idea."

"No idea of what?"

Lindsey jumped and turned to find Walker right behind her, crowding her into the tree. "No idea what you were doing in here. That you were so talented. Walker, this is . . . incredible." The last word came out on a whisper as his eyes darkened and his head tipped closer to hers. She didn't think about the potential weirdness, she just thought about how much she wanted it. She stood up on her toes and leaned a hand against his chest and he leaned down to close the gap between their mouths and he was kissing her.

*   *   *

Nobody came into his garage when he was working. That was a hard and fast rule. Even Myron stayed out until he was invited.

But it was hard for Walker to think about Myron when he was holding onto Lindsey like he was a drowning man looking for a metaphor. He didn't want to take her to bed. He just wanted to throttle her, then change the locks on the garage.

But then she pressed up closer and opened her mouth, and his tongue seized the opportunity.

God, she felt good. It was like her wholesomeness was rubbing off on him, or maybe it was just her leg. Either way, he was so glad that he had decided to stop blaming her for his problems and to try to be nice. This was nice. A handful of those shorts was definitely nice.

She must have felt it, too, because her hands snaked up his shoulders and wound their way into his hair. He hitched her up closer and she made a little sound. He hoped it was a good sound, and then he knew it was a good sound because she wrapped her legs around him and he did a mental scan of his garage for the safest place to put her so he could press her even closer.

He took half a step toward his workbench with a vague thought of sweeping hundreds of dollars of tools to the ground. But that half a step must have broken the spell because suddenly Lindsey pulled back and was squirming, which at first he liked. But then he realized she was squirming to get down. So he eased her gently down his body, holding onto her hips until her feet touched the ground.

Then he saw her face.

Mother Teresa was not happy.

"What the hell?" she said as she swiped a hand across her mouth.

Walker instantly had that old feeling in his gut, the one that felt like he had swallowed a rock and it was bringing him down, guts first. His palms started to sweat. He opened his mouth to apologize. Really, what had he been thinking, grabbing her like that? And he'd thought she had responded to his kiss, but maybe that was wrong too. Maybe that was what he'd felt because that was what he wanted to feel. His panicked thoughts tripped over each other, tying his tongue so all he could do was stupidly stare.

"I'm sorry," Lindsey said, finally.

His head shot up. She was sorry? For him mauling her?

"I shouldn't have come in here. And I know it's not much of an apology, but I was so angry. I wanted revenge."

He opened his mouth, but Lindsey beat him to it.

"I can't believe you did that."

He couldn't believe it either. Sure, he'd been wanting to do that ever since he'd seen her scolding the garden into growing in those cute little shorts. But that didn't mean . . . he suddenly realized that she was not talking about the kiss.

"If you didn't want me to have people over, you could have just said something."

Have people over? He wasn't upset about that. No, he thought, his shame slowly morphing into indignation, he didn't care about her social life, not anymore. He just didn't want her trespassing in his locked studio.

"Did you have to tear up the entire garden?"

Wha?

"That was Myron's garden. Or is it because you said it was mine now, so it doesn't mean anything?"

He watched her lips quiver and her eyes blinking fast. Oh god, he thought. I kissed Mother Teresa and then I made her cry.

"I knew you were rude. I had no idea you were cruel."

"What are you—?" he started, reaching for her.

She jerked her arm away. "Don't touch me. I can't believe you!" she screeched.

He held his hands up, surrendering. "What do you mean about the garden?"

She froze for a second, and Walker felt the daggers of her stare go right through his heart. Then she tore the door open and stomped out.

He followed her out. He wanted to defend himself. She wasn't mad at him for the reason he thought. She was mad at him for something else entirely, something that she would not explain. But she wouldn't slow down and talk, and now he was starting to get mad.

It was a hell of a way to end a kiss.

She stopped halfway up the path that led to the house. She stood there, hands on her hips, looking out over the garden.

It was a crazy torn up mess. He'd vaguely registered this on the way to the garage, but what did he know about gardening?

She flung her arm out over the mess. "You're telling me you didn't do this in some midnight rampage?"

Was that what she thought of him? Mother Teresa had some funny ideas about how to be a good landlord. "Why would I destroy my own yard?"

"Because you hate me for having fun and making friends and trying to be nice to you!"

He watched her take a deep breath and gaze up at the sky as if she was looking for help or answers or lightning to strike him.

"So you didn't destroy the garden?" she asked.

"No," he said firmly, crossing his arms over his chest.

"So someone broke in in the middle of the night while you were out in your garage working and destroyed the garden."

"I guess so."

"Maybe because you were blasting bad heavy metal all night?"

"Hey, it's not bad. It's Iron Maiden."

She waved her hand. "Whatever. Your golden oldies."

"Maybe," he said, letting the oldies go.

"So, either you did it, or someone did it because of you. Either way, your fault."

That was a funny kind of logic. But she looked so angry, he didn't push her.

He just stared her down.

"You are a ridiculous human being," she said, and stomped into the house.

Well, he wasn't going to argue with her on that.

He stomped into his side of the house.

Oops.

Chapter 11

Lindsey heard Walker's door slam. She leaned against her own recently slammed door and hung her head. It was just a little patch of plants. It wasn't even hers, not yet, anyway. She'd spent a few weeks weeding it. It was her own fault for getting so excited about it. Who got so excited about home-grown produce, anyway?

It was the move, that's all. The move and the stress of all the change and the hangover and the hot kiss. That was a lot for a girl to handle.

But what hurt the most was Walker's cruelty. That he could be so spiteful, to destroy something she cared about just because he was angry. And before she even had a chance to find out that he was angry! That man needed some communication lessons.

He said he hadn't done it. She didn't believe him, but he really looked like he hadn't noticed the destruction. Her Detective kicked in, and she started to see clues. The garden was pretty thoroughly torn up, but he didn't seem to have any dirt on him. Oh, he was dirty, and he smelled like sweat and metal—she had gotten close enough to find that out. But surely he would've had some dirt on his clothes if he'd spent half the night throwing plants around?

She definitely would have noticed the dirt. She noticed all of his smells. The tang of sweat and metal. She also noticed the feel of his hair, like silk around her fingers. And his shoulders, and the vise-like grip of his arms around her ribs. But a gentle vise. A nice vise.

She shivered. That was some kiss. It almost made her forget that she hated him right now.

But that kiss, and that art. Any man who could create like that and kiss like that was a man with some serious depth. The more he kept that depth from her, hidden behind half-frowns and exasperated silence, the more she wanted to break down those walls.

So if he hadn't destroyed the garden, who had?

If she couldn't figure out the mystery of Walker's hidden depths, she could at least figure out who was crazy enough to pull their yard apart in the middle of the night.

She opened the door and poked her head out, noting that Walker's door was still slammed shut. She felt like an idiot, especially as she crept, Pink Panther-style, toward the garden, but she couldn't help it. Something was up, and she needed to know what it was.

She stood up and surveyed the damage. Yup, pretty damaged. But there was a tomato plant that was encased in one of those circle wire-y cage things that seemed to have survived. And as she stepped into the garden, she saw that at least one of the zucchini plants was still intact. At least she thought it was a zucchini plant. She should have brought her book out with her.

Because that would not have been dorky at all. First sleuthing, then with a reference book.

Made it hard to believe Walker had wanted to kiss her at all.

She shook that thought off. He hadn't wanted to kiss her. He had just done it to distract her from his top-secret work-in-progress.

Even though, toward the end there, he wasn't exactly acting like a man who was just trying for a distraction. One does not simply squeeze a girl's butt like that if one only wants a distraction.

But his distraction was distracting her from her investigation. Clues. She needed clues. Maybe he had stuff in the garage that she could use to make a mold of any footprints she found. Then she could compare it to the shoes people in the neighborhood owned, and then . . .

She was sidetracked by a rustle at the side of the garage, the one closest to where she stood in the garden. *Aha,* she thought. *The culprit is back for more.* "Come on out, buddy," she said, and picked up the nearest weapon. Which, unfortunately, was her dead eggplant.

Well, at least she would die defending her territory. She watched the unmown grass wave as whatever was hiding moved closer to her. She took a step forward and the waving stopped, but she only had to wait a second for it to start up again. Then she heard a snap and a squeak and the grass went crazy as the beast sprang from its hiding place and charged straight toward Lindsey.

Before she had a chance to throw down her useless weapon and run, she was knocked into the garden, taking the last tomato plant with her. She grabbed for her attacker, pulling it off of her and—

It was a puppy. A big, brown, wet-nosed puppy, whining and burrowing into her armpit. He seemed upset, and Lindsey saw why—his tail was clamped in a mousetrap, one of those old-fashioned metal-and-wood ones.

"Okay, okay," she said in as soothing a voice as she could muster, what with her heart beating out of her chest. "Hold on, pup. I've got it." She grabbed the wooden bottom of the trap with one hand and his tail with the other, and the dog whimpered and jerked and almost blew out Lindsey's ear drum with a high-pitched yelp, but the mousetrap came off. Lindsey tossed the thing aside and dropped her head into the dirt. The puppy sat on her chest and licked her nose.

"Uh, you're welcome," she said, then scratched behind his ears.

"What's that?" Walker asked when he came back to find Lindsey not quite where he left her.

Lindsey looked up from whatever she was doing on the ground in what was left of her garden and held her arms out. Her arms, which were full of dog.

"It's a dog."

He shook his head. "I know that. I can see that. But . . . why?"

"Well," she said, "when a mommy dog and a daddy dog love each other very much . . ."

He noticed the mischievous glint in her eye. He was still annoyed at her.

"What is it doing here?"

"I think he's hungry." Walker watched blankly as the dog licked Lindsey's face. "I think he's the garden destroyer."

"That little dog did all this?" Walker didn't know much about dogs. He never had one. This dog looked way too small to be able to tear up every square inch of garden.

Although the dog's feet were pretty big. If his feet were any indication of his appetite, then . . . maybe.

The dog wiggled out of Lindsey's arms and made his somersaulting-over-his-ears way to Walker. "This dog must be part Tasmanian devil." He watched as the dog bounced up and down on Walker's knee.

"He had all night." Lindsey shrugged, then knelt down to pick up the dog. "Didn't you, my little love machine angel baby face." She shrieked and laughed as he licked her.

"Wait a second." Walker crossed his arms over his chest, refusing to be charmed by either Pollyanna or her Destroying Angel. "When you thought I tore up the garden, you were pissed."

"Yeah," she said, clearly only half-listening to him as the dog tried to climb up her chest and nip at her ponytail.

"So why is the dog off the hook?"

She looked at him sharply. "The dog can't help it! He doesn't know any better! Besides, he was probably starving!"

"So if I was starving and tore up your garden, you would be fine with it?"

She threw him a challenging glare. "If you were as cute as the dog is."

"Hey, I'm—" Walker stopped himself. He was *not* cute.

He threw his arms up. "Fine. The dog wins. Whose dog is it, anyway?"

"I don't know. He doesn't have a collar." Lindsey scratched behind the dog's ears. He flopped onto his belly at her feet. Lucky dog. "But he did have this attached to his tail."

She held up one of those ancient cartoon-style mousetraps Myron had insisted on putting around the garage. Those had been out there for years. Walker thought he'd picked them all up. He was surprised he hadn't stepped on it the last time he mowed the lawn.

Good thing he didn't mow the lawn very often.

"How could you?" Lindsey spat at him, and pulled the dog closer to her chest.

"I didn't mean to trap the dog! Although you should be thanking me. Without that trap, you never would have caught him."

"Hmph." She held up the dog's face and started speaking baby-talk gibberish to him.

Walker rubbed his jaw. "So, how are you going to find his owner?"

Lindsey huffed out a breath. "I guess we have to find your home, don't we, boy? I'll make some posters. Here," she said, handing the dog to Walker. "Hold him while I get my phone."

Before Walker could say anything, he had his hands full of dog, and Lindsey was sprinting into the house. The dog was still dangling from Walker's hands when she came out, phone in hand.

"Hold him up so I can get his face. Oh my gosh, support his legs," Lindsey scolded him. "He's not going to bite."

"He could bite," muttered Walker.

"Over here! Look over here, boy! That's a good boy!" Lindsey made a series of clicking and whistling noises that the dog ignored. Instead, he just licked Walker's hands.

"You know . . ." he said, and pulled the dog tight to him with one hand while he wiped the other on his jeans.

"Got it! Very cute. Oh my gosh, Walker, you're smiling in this one! It's a miracle!"

What was that supposed to mean? "Hey, why am I in the picture?"

She shrugged. "I'll crop you out. Look at this face." She tapped her phone to zoom in on the dog's face, his big brown eyes glistening pathetically and adorably in the sun. Lindsey smelled like sweat and peppermint. The dog licked her cheek.

Lucky dog.

"We'll find your home, don't you worry," she said, snuffling her nose into the dog's neck. Walker just stood there, trying hard not to inhale the scent of her hair or generally drool over the good feeling he got when she was near. He also tried not to be jealous of the dog. Because it was a dog.

This dog, he thought as it wormed its way out from under Lindsey's affection to rest its chin on Walker's shoulder, *this dog is a problem.*

"Oh my god, do not move," she said and circled around them, phone out. "Holy crap. I can't . . . Okay, my ovaries just exploded."

Walker turned at that, despite her instruction. She stuck the phone in his face again. "Please," she said, and he just grunted because, please what? The dog was flopped in sleep on his shoulder. It was pretty cute. If Walker had ovaries, he imagined they'd be exploding right now, too.

Until he felt the picturesque, adorable, ovary-exploding drool soak through the shoulder of his shirt.

Why was he letting this dog drool on his shirt again?

Lindsey stood in front of him, swiping at her phone as her face morphed into various stages of maniacal joy.

That's why. He was covered in dog drool because watching this woman's gloriously joyful face made it worthwhile.

He'd been covered in worse.

He had it bad for Lindsey. He should go inside and put his house on the market and not come out until he had a moving truck lined up. He did not like the idea of pining over his next-door neighbor.

He never should have kissed her.

Myron was going to have a field day with this.

With a sigh, Lindsey looked up from her phone. The look she gave him was slightly less joyous, but it was a hell of a lot better than the one she'd given him when she thought he'd torn up her garden.

"I guess you're off the hook," she said.

He was standing in the middle of a destroyed vegetable garden, his work left unfinished and exposed in the garage, a drooling puppy on his shoulder that he didn't want to put down because it made Lindsey happy and, if it was internal monologue confession time, he kind of liked the warm, furry weight.

All in all, not the worst situation he'd ever been in. But Walker felt decidedly on the hook.

"For the garden," Lindsey clarified. "Clearly it wasn't you."

It rankled that she ever thought it might be. But then the puppy shifted and Lindsey came over to scratch behind its ears and Walker smelled her again and he was done rankling for the moment.

"Thanks for the vote of confidence," he said with as much sarcasm as he could muster in the face of her sincerity and her aroma.

She narrowed her eyes at him. "I'm still not sleeping with you, you know."

The puppy squirmed out of his arms and reached an adorable tongue over to lick Lindsey's hands. She giggled and baby-talked and reached over to pull the dog off Walker.

He was finally rid of the burden of the garden-destroying beast, but that wasn't what made him smile. "You were thinking of sleeping with me?"

She tossed him another narrowed-eye glare, the ferocity of which was slightly marred by the rosy blush that crept into her cheeks.

He was still probably going to have to move. But she was thinking of sleeping with him.

He was pathetic.

And he wasn't going to sleep with her.

But he was smiling.

Chapter 12

"I'm still not sleeping with you."

Lindsey cringed at the memory, even weeks later. But at least it had led to a truce. She had a truce, and she had a dog. It was official. The morning of the Garden Incident she'd called Billie, who got her an appointment with the vet (who was also Katie's brother and Grace's fiancé's cousin—small towns). Keith confirmed that the dog was about six months old, a little undernourished but healthy enough to neuter, and not microchipped. So Lindsey had him snipped and vaccinated, and made posters with Walker's face cropped out. She hung them everywhere—in Hollow Bend, where Keith's practice was, around Willow Springs, on the Pembroke campus. As one week turned into two, she gave up on holding back hope that the dog would go unclaimed, and started thinking about a name.

She wasn't going to sleep with Walker, but at least she had a dog.

The dog was surprisingly good when she was out of the house. It was only when she was home that he would find shoelaces and unroll the toilet paper and just generally wreak the most adorable havoc ever. But when she left him alone, he was fine. She created a little nest for him in the laundry room, and closed the door while at work to keep him contained. Every day, so far, she came home to an undestroyed laundry room and a dog that would wiggle himself off-balance, he was so happy to see her.

And one of her secret childhood dreams came true—falling asleep to the warm weight of a sleeping ball of fur nestled against her.

So much better than sleeping with Walker.

Walker stopped, poised over his kitchen sink, and listened to the front door close. He quit loading the dishwasher and headed for the laundry room. He knew he had exactly forty-five seconds before the howling and crying.

Lindsey didn't use the chain on her side of the laundry room door. Walker discovered this the first time he went into her house uninvited, rushing past that big blue couch to get to her laundry room. That first day, the dog barked happily at him, which was a big improvement over the heartbreaking, ear-splitting whining.

So now, Walker just held open the door, and the little booger came rushing into his apartment, where he began a long day of following Walker around.

Walker wasn't home when Lindsey got back from work. Or at least his truck wasn't parked in the driveway, which, so far, had meant that he wasn't home. Not that she was stalking him.

But her dog was there. Her cute, floppy, unnamed dog was there, whining until she opened the laundry room door, where he launched himself into her arms, then out the back door.

She grabbed a quick snack, then took the dog for a long walk. When they got back about an hour later, he was pooped, which had been the idea.

"Now you listen to me," she said, getting down to puppy level. "I'm going out to dinner with Grace. But I promise I'll be back soon and I will give you t-r-e-a-t-s. Okay? Okay? Is that okay? Are you my lovey face? Is that okay, my lovey face?"

It was okay, although Lindsey had to close her eyes against the sad puppy dog face as she shut the laundry room door.

Why did she close the door? I don't like when she closes the door. Is she ever even coming back? I love her. I don't want her to leave me. I already smelled everything in this room. That one spot smells good. I'll smell it again and maybe take a drink. When is she coming back? This floor is cold except for this soft spot but should I sit on it or chew on it? Hey, wait a second. I hear something. What is that sound? Is she coming back? No it's coming from over here. I have to get to it because what if she never comes back or maybe she's over there and she forgot about me? I better get over there because what if she forgets to give me dinner? I just know she's right over there. Hold on, I'm coming. Hold on, I'm coming, I'm coming, I'm coming!

*   *   *

Lindsey did her best not to break land speed records on her way home. She was now officially the worst dinner date in town, although Grace had been just as distracted as Lindsey was. Except Grace was worried about professional travel fellowships and research papers. Lindsey was worried that her dog would miss her.

Grace didn't get it. Grace had a cat. Cats don't miss you, she told Lindsey. They just tell you that you never should have left in the first place.

But it was still a nice dinner, and the idea of a weekend movie was floated around. Friends! Lindsey had friends now.

Friends and a dog who loved her. A dog who would wag his tail and jump up to lick her face and . . .

"Oh, shit."

Walker pulled into the driveway but sat in his truck for a minute. The days were getting longer. It was summer. He had gone to the woods to visit his tree, then lost track of time wandering. The sun had set behind him as he drove out of the forest, and he was starving. But he was also itching to work. He'd just decided to work first, eat later, when he saw the lights in his bedroom go on.

He wasn't home. Why were the lights on?

He let himself in quietly, through the front door. He grabbed the nearest weapon, which was a magazine. No problem, as long as the intruder was a fly. He could hear Lindsey next door, talking to the dog, and he moved a little faster. If there was someone in his apartment, she could be in danger too.

When he got to his bedroom, though, there was nobody there.

Not anymore, anyway.

He hadn't made his bed that morning, but he definitely hadn't left his sheets in a tangle on the floor. And he absolutely hadn't chewed up his pillows so there was stuffing everywhere.

There didn't seem to be a thing in his room that was not chewed on. Tennis shoes, books, the legs of the old leather armchair, the dirty clothes he had thrown over the old leather armchair.

Dammit, she'd promised she would lock that thing up. How had the dog gotten in here, anyway?

He heard a sharp bark from his kitchen, and Lindsey's raised voice. How did *she* get in here?

As soon as he rounded the corner from the stairs, it was clear.

Clear as the hole in the laundry room door, the one that led straight through to Lindsey's apartment.

"Hi," she said sheepishly, leaning down to peek through what was left of the door. The dog squirmed in her arms and escaped, launching himself at Walker.

"I'm so sorry." She climbed through the door—what was left of the door, and bent down to try to corral the dog, who was trying to climb Walker.

"What the—" He couldn't even find the words to express his . . . his what? His anger? His shock? How did a dog that little eat that much door?

She stood up, leaving the dog to chew on Walker's shoelaces.

"He's so good when I leave him for work, so I thought he'd be fine if I went out to dinner . . ." Her voice trailed off at the end as she pointed toward the chewed-up door. "At least he didn't damage any electric stuff?"

Walker had a sudden image of the dog chewing on a wire, then flying across the room.

He scooped the dog up in his arms. Just to get him to stop chewing on his shoelaces.

"I'm really, really sorry. I'll pay for the door. I'll get a new door. You don't even have to do anything. I'll bring the dog to work—"

He took a step back as she reached for the dog. "If he chews through a door"—Walker still couldn't believe that this little beast had chewed through a *door*—"what kind of damage do you think he'll do in a nursing home?"

"I know, but—"

"And don't you think you should take him to the vet? Since he just ate a door?"

"Yes! Of course! I left a message!" She held up her phone, then reached for the dog again.

"You locked him up all day, then left him again? So you could go out to dinner?"

She looked at him, puzzled. "I was barely gone for an hour."

"I just—" Walker stopped himself before he could say, "I just don't think you're ready for a dog." That's what Red used to say, no matter how much Walker kept up with his chores or did as he was told. He could have been ready for a dog. He would have been ready for a dog, if they didn't move so damn much.

Besides, he knew Lindsey took care of the little booger. He knew she devoted all the time she wasn't at work to making sure he ate and got exercise, and she'd spent almost three hours outside with him last weekend and he was finally, usually, sitting on command. It definitely wasn't helping Booger's separation anxiety that Walker went and fetched him every day.

"I can take him," he said, his brain working fast.

"What?"

"When you go out. He can hang out with me."

"All day? While I'm at work?"

Walker shrugged. What a great idea he had just completely and spontaneously come up with.

"But what if you have to . . . I don't know, go sculpt somewhere?"

"You mean besides my studio?"

She shrugged. "I can't ask you to do that."

"It's better than . . ." He waved a hand at the door.

"Okay," she said slowly. "Okay, that will be nice." She reached over and petted the dog's head. "He seems okay." She lifted his chin and looked into his eyes, then started feeling down the dog's body. The dog wiggled, but Walker thought it was more in delight than in pain.

Lucky dog.

She was close again, so close that her hair tickled his chin. It smelled like herbs and lemons. Just as he was about to take a deep, embarrassing breath, she looked up. They stood there, staring at each other, a squirming Booger between them. She leaned up. He leaned down.

The phone rang in her hand.

"That's probably the vet," she said, and disappeared through the hole in the door.

"Good news," Lindsey said as she climbed back through the door. "You don't have to—"

But the good news was lost in a blast of surprise and glee at the sight that greeted her: Walker, on his knees, his fine butt in the air, playing tug of war with the dog and a T-shirt. In his mouth.

He was growling.

At the dog.

The moment was so perfect and so strange, so much better than any cute scenario she ever could have imagined, that she almost cried. Instead, she just stood still, mouth open around the good news, and soaked the silliness in before Walker noticed her.

It didn't take long.

He opened his mouth to let go of the shirt, and the dog went tumbling backward, tangled up in victory.

"It's clean," he said, and wiped his mouth.

She shrugged, like it was no big deal, like she wouldn't be re-living that moment randomly throughout the next week and laughing. "I can't believe you let the dog win."

The dog had untangled himself from the shirt and was climbing up Walker's lap—lucky dog—shaking the T-shirt at him, taunting him with another round.

Walker grabbed one end of the shirt, but didn't pull. "What did Keith say?"

"Just to keep an eye on him, make sure he's not acting like he's in pain."

The dog was now flopped on his back on the floor, belly exposed to Walker's vigorous rubbing.

Lucky dog.

"I think he's fine for now," she said, and kneeled on the floor next to Walker. She took one end of the shirt and waved it over the dog's head. He jumped up, pounced, and took off for a lap around the room. "Sorry. I hope you didn't want that shirt."

But Walker wasn't looking at the shirt. He was looking at her, and before she knew it they were locked in another moment just like the one before Keith called. She just had to tilt her head up, lean into him a little, and they could be kissing.

And this would be a real kiss, not a stupid spontaneous reaction to a bad situation. She leaned in, and he leaned in, bracing his hand on the floor behind her. She almost lost her balance, so she grabbed his shoulder, then his other hand was around her waist, holding her up. They never broke eye contact, not until she closed her eyes and finally pressed her mouth to his. His arms went around her and squeezed and her spine straightened and she aligned herself more fully with him, chest to chest, and she gasped as she felt his fingers dig into her rear and his tongue slide into her mouth. Then he stood up, taking her with him, and then his hands went lower, cupping her butt, then the backs of her thighs and she trusted his strength and let him lift her legs so they wrapped around his hips. He backed her up until she hit something, an end table maybe, because then she was perched on it and his hands were roaming everywhere. He was rough. No, not rough, he was thorough. No part of her back or her thighs or her neck went untouched. Then he moved to her front and she let out a feral groan as he cupped her breasts.

He stepped back suddenly, his hand still on her breast.

"Are you okay?" he asked, breathlessly.

She gave him an impatient look. "What?"

"I thought I—" he jerked his hand away. "Sorry."

No way, not this again, she thought, and she crossed her ankles and pulled his hips closer. He still looked like he had something to say, so she reached down and pulled her shirt over her head and he might have said something, but his face was buried in her bra so she really didn't care. He spun her away from the wall, then stopped. He looked like he was trying to make a decision.

"Couch?" she suggested, remembering the state her dog had left his bed in. He nodded and in two steps she was down on her back and he was on top of her, his hips grinding against hers through their jeans.

Jeans. Stupid jeans. She reached between them for the button on his while he sat up and pulled his shirt off and, holy god, up close he was even better. He smiled and leaned down to kiss her but she held him back. "I need a moment," she said, and ran her hands over the planes of his chest, the ridges of his abs, his smooth sides. His breathing got heavier, but then he started to look embarrassed so she sat up real quick and undid her bra so he wouldn't be the only one without a shirt on.

"Holy god," he whispered, and his rough hands were gentle on her sensitive skin, his calloused fingers running over her nipples, tracing a circle under her breasts.

She managed to arch herself into his hands and get his jeans down over his hips at the same time. She was feeling very impressed with herself, and then she was just feeling Walker, hard and hot against her thigh. She reached down and he cursed into her neck.

"Lindsey," he whispered and she melted. Then he cursed and twisted around, digging at his feet into the pocket of his jeans. He tangled and lost his balance, his knees still straddling her on the couch, one hand holding himself up off the floor.

She giggled, and he gave her a teasing look. "Come on," she said and scrambled out from underneath him, then pushed him down so his back was on the couch, his head propped against the arm. She climbed over him, took the condom from his hand, and tore the wrapper with her teeth, just like in the movies. She slid the condom down over him in one smooth move and he was hot and hard in her hand and she couldn't wait, and didn't think he needed her to wait, so she positioned herself above him and went to work.

"Oh my god," he said as she slid over him. She wanted to revel in her triumph over his grumpiness, but then she was full of Walker and she couldn't do anything but throw her head back and gasp. He gripped her hips, moving her as he moved, and her spine stopped working and she had to prop her hands on his chest, and the shift in position felt so good that she had to lean her whole chest against his, the rough hair abrading her breasts as he rocked her.

And, holy crap, he rocked her. Then he lifted up a knee, just a little, just enough to change his angle and she reared back, surprised and breathless, and she screamed and flew over the edge. Walker gripped her hips even tighter and bucked hard under her, once, twice, then he groaned and she tightened and collapsed on top of him.

She let out a breathless laugh. She'd known her persistence would pay off. She'd known it would be worth it to get Walker out of his shell.

The lady was great. She smelled really nice and she loved to hold him and pet him and play with him. At first the lady was his favorite. But then the guy played with him and gave him snacks and he had even more interesting smells that he had to dig real deep to find. So now he couldn't decide who he liked better. Good thing he got rid of that door, so he didn't have to choose.

Chapter 13

"Nice place."

It wasn't the messiest his apartment had ever been, but it was pretty bad. Walker suddenly wished he'd picked up a little.

In his defense, he didn't know that Jake Burdette was coming over. Not until Jake rang the bell and told him he had a door for him.

Walker tried to look at his apartment through Jake's eyes. Big furniture—he liked to nap. And a big couch was good for a lot of things. A giant afghan Darlene had made for him. Shoes everywhere, which was a bad habit he had to break, especially since most of those shoes were now missing laces, thanks to Booger.

It wasn't great, but it was home.

"Lots of good light in here." Jake knocked on the walls, looked at the doorframes. "Solid. How long have you had this place?"

"Couple years."

"Ever think about making it a single-family home?"

Walker thought about waking up with Lindsey wrapped around him after they moved to her bed for round two.

Which had nothing to do with construction projects.

He just liked thinking about her wrapped around him.

To Jake, he just shrugged, and continued to show him around.

It was weird standing in his kitchen, talking to Jake Burdette about normal guy stuff. Walker hadn't seen Jake since freshman year of high school, when they both went out for the basketball team. Walker had a few inches on Jake, but Jake was faster. He remembered it clearly: Jake faking and swerving around the defense, Walker raising his arms and blocking the shot.

He remembered all of his time in Willow Springs.

Hell, that was why he came back. It was one of the best places he and Red had lived, where the kids were more curious than cruel to the big, gangly new kid. Where he actually lived with his dad, not that he saw him much. But by that time, Walker was getting old enough to be sick of Red's informal relationship with the truth, so that worked out just fine. Walker cooked rice and beans, like Mrs. Garcia had taught him. He mostly did his homework, and went out for basketball.

And he made the team. He did, Jake didn't. Walker had thought that was unfair, that he had only made it because of his "wingspan," as the coach called it.

But it didn't matter, because a few weeks later, he and Red were on the road. Walker always wondered if Jake got his spot on the team.

He could ask him. They were sitting around, talking like guys.

"Is this the destroyer?"

"Dammit, Booger!" Walker tried to keep hold of the dog's collar as his giant paws made a lunge for Jake.

"It's okay," Jake said. Then, *oof*. "He's gonna be big. Look at these feet."

"And he's got an appetite."

"You're a real tough guy, you know that?" And now Jake was on the floor, roughhousing with the dog.

Finally, Jake stood up and stretched a hand toward Walker.

"So. Welcome back."

"Uh. Thanks."

"Been a while, huh?"

Yup, thought Walker. *It's been a while since my dad faked some Civil War-era paintings and we had to skip town.*

"Sorry I haven't come by sooner. Grace thinks I should've shown up with a gift basket."

"Grace?"

"Fiancée. Wife, soon, but she doesn't want to plan a wedding so we both keep putting it off."

"Why don't you elope?"

"Her sister and my sister have threatened bodily harm if we do."

"Hmm." Walker couldn't even imagine what life would've been like with siblings. Everyone he knew talked like sisters and brothers were the worst thing in the world, but in a way that made it clear to Walker they were actually the best. But to have another kid grow up like Walker? Would a sister have made watching late-night motel TV more fun than it was?

"So what have you been up to? Grace tells me you're a big-time artist now."

"Not big-time."

"Well, you got you a palace here," Jake said, and gave him a friendly punch on the shoulder. "And I got you a door. Just pretend there's a bow on it, for Grace's sake."

"Yeah, okay. Dog proof?"

"Normally I'd say yes, but your dog seems to be a door-eating savant."

"Not my dog."

Walker saw Jake's eyebrow raise as Booger ran insane circles around the two of them.

"Forget it. Let's get this door."

And now there's another guy! He smells like a cat, which isn't great, but he's a lot of fun and he's really impressed with how fast I can run around in circles. Hey, wait. Where are you going? Oh, whew, he's back. What's that big thing he's holding? Where are they going with that?

Oh, no . . .

Jake grunted as he tried to shove the door into place. "I've installed easier doors."

It wasn't helping that every time Booger scratched on the bedroom door, Walker had a little panic that he was going to break free. He didn't think Jake's housewarming generosity would extend to a second replacement door. And he definitely wanted this door replaced. This was a two-family house. Lindsey needed her space; he needed his. Sometimes they could share space, but that would be optional, with the option to close the door.

"I gotta be honest with you," Jake said. "Grace put me up to this."

"Grace sent you to fix the door?" How did she even know?

"No, Lindsey sent me for the door. Grace sent me to find out the dirt on you. She's dying of curiosity. It killed her when she came over the other night and couldn't get into your studio."

Walker hadn't actually met Grace, but he'd seen her at the gallery on campus. He'd been attempting to unobtrusively look at the exhibit of Appalachian landscape photography from the 1930s. She was in there with a class, talking about post-modernism. He recognized her laugh.

He wanted to tell Jake that if she'd waited around long enough, Lindsey could have snuck her in. Not that he really minded that anymore. Especially not since he started sneaking into her apartment to kidnap her dog.

No, the idea of Lindsey in his studio didn't bother him as much as it should have. He was probably still high from last night. And this morning. "Not you?" he asked Jake. "You're not curious?"

"I don't really care what you do, man. As long as it's not illegal." Jake looked at him sharply. "It's not illegal, is it?"

"No, it's not . . . it's hard to explain." Hard to explain that he was a pretty famous artist but he was protective to the point of paranoia about his work because he used to help his dad make a living by faking art. And the only person he'd let into the garage was Myron. And now Lindsey. And, recently and regularly, the dog.

"Just don't blow up the neighborhood," Jake said, slapping him on the back. He gave the door a push. "This oughta hold. Feed the dog real food, okay?"

"Hey." Walker threw his hands up. "Not my dog."

Chapter 14

"So now you have a dog?"

Myron sat on the bench inside the wire fence of the dog park making faces at the slimy tennis ball that Booger kept dropping at his feet.

"It's Lindsey's dog," Walker told him, picking up the ball and tossing it to the other end of the park. The dog took off like a shot after it, not letting a little thing like tripping over his own feet stop him from reaching his target.

"Sure don't look like Lindsey's dog."

"She can't exactly bring the dog to work."

"Why not? He doesn't slobber near as much as Eugene does."

"Ha ha." Walker tossed the ball again.

Booger went nuts after it.

"So what's really bothering you?"

"Nothing. It's a nice day. I thought you'd like to get out, that's all."

"It's a nice day at Shady Grove and I don't step in dog poop there."

"I told you, that's just mud."

"And you've got that assy face again."

Walker tossed the ball one more time, but Booger was too involved in something under the doggy slide. Walker sat down next to Myron.

"My dad called. This morning, after..." Walker wasn't sure he wanted to explain about the door and Jake. It was complicated. Never mind last night, and the complications he had created with Lindsey.

"Ah. What's he want?"

"Nothing, he said. Just wanted to tell me he's getting out."

"Oh yeah? He's a free man after ten years and he wants nothing from you?"

"He wants to come visit, see what I'm working on."

"Huh."

"I didn't tell him where I am, and I didn't invite him. But he's Red, so I'm kind of expecting him to show up any minute."

"I'd be interested in seeing him again."

Walker gave Myron an eyebrow. "I'm not sure that's a good idea."

"What's he gonna do, swindle me out of my money? No problem. I ain't got any."

"I just think . . . the further he stays away, the better."

"Well, if he bothers you, you can sic your dog on him."

"Not my dog," Walker said. Booger rolled in the mud, then chased his tail.

Chapter 15

This day needed to be over.

Without her ending up in a car wreck.

Lindsey rolled down the windows, but the hot summer night air was doing nothing to help keep her awake. Just one more block . . .

Fortunately, the residual anxiety of the Worst Wednesday Ever kept her from drifting off the road. It had started rough. Ned Grubb apparently hadn't paid the bill for the institutional catering company they used, so Glen, their cook, had to run to the grocery store and get creative with eggs and canned fruit, and still her credit card would probably never recover. Then Eugene spent the morning flirting instead of eating and his blood sugar dropped, and nothing ruined a sunny day at a nursing home faster than someone being taken away in an ambulance. The fact that he was fine did not reduce the amount of paperwork she had to do.

Then Lindsey spent hours on the phone, first trying to reach Eugene's daughter, then trying to calm her down enough that she could safely drive to see her father. Then Evan called and said he had strep, and there was no way Lindsey was letting any of those germs near Shady Grove, so she ended up working a double, which meant she also had to stay for the Willow Springs Middle School Chorus on their annual "sing to the old people concert," as Evan called it. Not that Lindsey didn't love a good show tunes medley. She just . . . she was tired. Tired and strangely wired.

Lindsey sat in the driveway, not ready to face more of real life.

Real life meant a dog that needed to be walked, although she'd managed a moment to text Walker to ask him to feed him. She also had to feed herself, and Willow Springs was sorely lacking in takeout options. What she really wanted was a glass of wine and someone to take her mind off her Wednesday from Hell. She let herself in and saw the light on in the garage.

Walker glanced up toward the corner. She was still there. But now she'd found a stool and was perched, elbows on the drafting table, sipping a glass of wine. Still watching him.

"Am I making you self-conscious?"

"No," he said, suddenly very aware of how dirty his shirt was. "I'm still not used to an audience, that's all. This is not meant to be a performance."

"I don't want you to perform. I just like watching you." Booger got up from his bed in the corner (because, yes, Walker had put a dog bed in his studio) and sat at her feet. She idly leaned down to scratch behind his ears.

He cocked an eyebrow at her.

"In a just-friends way."

Walker grunted noncommittally. A lot of things she said sounded worse than she meant. It was part of what made listening to her so much fun.

"I mean, how do you know where to bend the thing or stick the thing to the thing?"

He raised his eyebrows.

"You know," she said, waving her hands vaguely tree-ward.

"I took some metalworking classes." Well, he took some after-school lessons from Myron. Close enough. He flicked his torch. "They don't let just anyone use these, you know." Actually, that wasn't true. But he was not a total dumbass, so he did learn how to use it properly first.

"I don't mean the technique. I mean, how do you know that moving this thing this way will make it look like this? Do you have a picture of it in your mind?"

"Yeah. And I have to sketch it out first. And I have to make sure it's balanced."

"Balanced? But this one is over here and that one is over there—" She must have been as tired as she looked. She was barely using words. He wouldn't have any idea what she was talking about if she wasn't pointing at the pieces of metal bark he was installing.

"I make sure the weight is balanced. Otherwise it'll topple over."

"And that's a whole different kind of sculpture." Booger put his paw on her lap, then climbed right up there. Without looking away from Walker's work, she opened her arms and let the dog snuggle in.

He smiled. "Exactly."

"So you sketch it, and then you just . . . make it?"

"Well, it's a little more complicated than that."

"But the sketch. Where does that come from? Do you just see it in your mind?"

"No." He saw her make a frustrated face. "Sort of. There's a tree I saw on a hike. It was dead, but it was huge. This huge, twisty tree had grown out of a rock, looking over the valley." He couldn't really explain it any better than that. He saw it, and now he was making it. And there was still that rush he got from creating, from shaping metal because he wanted to, because the metal wanted to, not because it had to look a certain way. But he didn't know how to explain that, exactly. He stood up and wiped his hands on a rag. "What are you getting at? What do you really want to know?"

"I don't know. I guess I'm just sort of fascinated by the fact that you can do this." She waved tree-ward.

"Thanks?"

"I don't mean it like that. I really meant it as a compliment. Don't you find it fascinating that people have such different gifts? That there are people in the world who can see things that no one else sees, and then can recreate them so other people can see them." She sipped her wine. "I am so tired. I'm not making any sense." She looked into her wine glass. "This probably isn't helping."

Walker looked at her. He was starting to appreciate her Pollyanna way of seeing things. He had never thought about his art as a particular gift. He just liked putting big metal pieces together, and people liked to buy the result. He never really thought about his vision being an extraordinary thing. Especially since he was raised by an artist who had no vision of his own.

Not that Red would admit that.

He turned and looked at the half-finished tree. He could see what it would become, for the most part. There would always be pieces that surprised him. That was part of what drove his compulsive welding binges, to get to that point of discovery.

Like that part, there. That needed to go. He put his gloves on and picked up a set of pliers and started peeling off parts of the bark.

"Now what are you doing?"

He jumped. He'd forgotten she was there.

"Sorry. Can you not work while I talk to you?"

He looked over his shoulder at her. "Would that stop you from talking?"

"Sure, yeah."

He turned back to the tree. "I'll believe that when I see it."

She was silent for a minute.

Just for a minute.

"When you hear it."

"What?"

"You'll believe it when you hear it, not see it. Or don't hear it, I guess. Because I won't be talking."

Walker didn't say anything.

"Okay, yes, I see what just happened. Ha ha, she can't stop talking. I'll go." She started to climb off the stool.

"No! No, you don't have to go. I was just teasing you."

"I don't want to interrupt."

"It's fine. Keep talking."

"You're making fun of me."

"I swear I'm not. I like your talking. Just, don't ask me so many questions."

"Just talk."

"Yeah."

"Just talk to myself?"

"No, talk to me."

"But don't expect an answer?"

Walker didn't answer.

"All I can think of are questions."

Walker sighed.

"How did you start?" Which was a question. She was tired . . . he should cut her some slack.

"What, you want my bio?"

"No. I already googled your bio. No picture."

"So?"

"It's just a shame."

Walker looked over at her. "Why?"

"No reason." She blushed. He smiled.

"What else did you learn?"

"You're an art school dropout and you're inspired by nature. Why'd you drop out of school?"

Walker shrugged and went back to the tree. "Ran out of money."

"Oh. But you bought a house."

"Yeah, because I stopped running out of money."

"But you didn't go back to school? Why not? Too cool?"

"Not cool enough."

"Hmm. And you'd have to deal with people. That's, like, your kryptonite."

Walker felt his face heat up. He focused on the tree.

She didn't say anything for a while, but he could feel that she was still there, watching him. It was kind of nice. She watched him like Myron did, just to watch. She didn't seem anxious about the finished product, just curious. There was no judgment in her gaze, no concern that what came out wouldn't be good enough.

Booger jumped off her lap and came over to sniff Walker's hands, but gave up when no pets were forthcoming. Walker saw him go back over to Lindsey and put his head on her knee. Puppy dog eyes were her kryptonite, obviously, because she started scratching behind his ears.

"This is hard."

Walker looked up at her, confused.

"Not talking," she explained.

"You can talk. I told you."

"I don't know what to talk about."

"All of the questions you want to ask me, answer them about yourself."

"Do I work out?"

He looked at her, confused. Then he remembered that first week, and that workout DVD. "I already know the answer to that question."

"Ha ha. Okay, where do I get my inspiration?"

"Sure."

She didn't say anything, and he looked over to see her nose wrinkled in confusion. "I don't know if 'inspiration' is the right word for what I do. I just like making people feel better. I don't mind blood. And I like old people. I don't really know why. When I was little, my Brownie troop did a service project at a nursing home, and I just fell in love with the people. Maybe it's because I don't have grandparents . . ."

She trailed off, and Walker looked up to see her staring dreamily at the ceiling.

"No grandparents?"

"They all died before I was born. Just me and my parents. I have an aunt somewhere, but she and my dad had some fight over my grandmother's will, so they don't speak. I don't even know if I have cousins. God, that's kind of sad."

Walker felt a small pang of jealousy. How lucky to feel wistful about not having contact with your family, instead of grateful.

She shrugged. "Geriatric nursing just seemed like a good fit. That's not a very exciting inspiration, is it?"

"People do things for much stranger reasons." Like forging art just because you can. "Sounds like you went into it because you love it. That's pretty good."

"Hmm. I never thought of it like that. I mean, I know I love it. But I thought I was just being practical."

She was quiet again, and he turned to see her staring vaguely into space, her head in her hand. He shook his head and went back to work.

He wasn't sure how many minutes passed, but she was quiet the whole time. It was a miracle. He found he sort of missed her jabber.

When he turned around again, though, he saw why she was quiet.

She was asleep with her head in her hand, the wine glass precariously close to the edge of the table.

He looked up at his tree, satisfied with what he accomplished tonight. There would always be more to do, but he had time. Tonight he had to put his sleepy Pollyanna to bed.

Lindsey woke up to a gentle jostling, and then Walker was in her face, blurry and smiling. She must have fallen asleep while he was working. She sat up straight, and she saw his hand snake out to grab her tilting wine glass.

"Good save," she told him. She rubbed her eyes and yawned.

"Come on, let's get you to bed," he told her, taking her arm gently.

"It's fine, I can do it." She hopped off the stool and tripped over Booger. If Walker hadn't been holding her arm, she would have landed on her face.

"Yup, you're fine."

"You stay and work." She patted his chest vaguely, tiredly.

"I don't trust you to make it inside without tripping over Booger again."

She let him guide her out of the garage, then took his arm and leaned her head against his shoulder as they walked into the house. When they got to the porch steps, she stopped. "Wait. Did you just call my dog Booger?"

He shrugged, and she could see from the light spilling out of her kitchen that he looked guilty. "It's not an insult. It just . . . it just sort of fit."

She looked down at her squirmy little puppy with the giant feet and the floppy ears. "Booger," she said. The pup looked up and barked.

"Unbelievable," she muttered.

Walker led her inside, where she tripped up the first step to the bedroom. He grabbed her around her waist, saving her face, but also igniting something inside of her.

"You gonna make it?" he asked from behind her, and she shook her head. So he took her hand and led her up the stairs and she let him pull her scrubs over her head and down her legs and watched as he pulled his shirt over his head and sat her down on the edge of the bed and knelt down, his shoulders strong between her thighs, and he took excellent care of her.

"So your dad's an art guy."

Walker was beginning to realize the many benefits of sleeping with Lindsey. She was generous, she was responsive, she was amazingly hot under that good-girl exterior. So far the only downside he could identify was afterward.

She wanted to talk.

Usually about him.

Walker said nothing.

"But not an artist," she said in that gently prodding way of hers.

"No." Red had talent, but Walker wouldn't call him an artist. His skills were more of mimicry than of original vision, although Red would argue that his vision *was* mimicry. That was Red's real strength: shaping the truth to suit his needs. Or at least shaping the appearance of the truth. And blaming the other guy whenever he did something wrong. "My dad . . . encouraged my art."

Especially when he discovered he might be able to make money from it.

"I thought your dad was a jerk?"

"He was. He is. He probably still is." Walker couldn't imagine that prison would have made Red more appealing in any way.

"But he encouraged your talent."

"No, he encouraged a way for him to make money off me."

"Hmm. It seems like if a parent wants to get rich off his kid, art should not be the field he pushes him into."

"He didn't care if I really made art. He just wanted to be able to sell it. Or, sell the idea of it."

"I don't get it." She really wouldn't let it go unless she could find the sunny side.

Well, he'd show her. There was no sunny side, which she would discover once she knew the whole story.

"He's in prison."

She sat up. "Why?"

"Wire fraud. He made a bunch of fake Civil War-era paintings and tried to pass them off as the real thing."

"Wow. And he got caught?"

"Eventually."

"Hmm. Seems like that wouldn't be a great way to make a living. How did it work more than once? Didn't people catch on?"

"He was always good at knowing when to skip town. Usually the gallery or shop would want to keep it quiet to protect their reputation, and he counted on that. We moved a lot."

"Oh." She tightened her hold around his chest, then let it go. "When I was growing up, I always wished we would move. Not because I didn't like Arizona—"

"Of course you did."

"Of course I did. I like everything." She pinched his side. "The new kids always seemed so . . . cool. They came from these other, exciting places. What was it like in those mysterious places they came from? What was sixth grade like in Indiana?"

Walker snorted. "You thought Indiana was exciting?"

"I've never been there. It might be exciting."

"You really were sheltered, weren't you?"

She rolled on top of him, pinning him to the mattress. "And that's why I live in exotic Kentucky."

"Lucky me."

"Damn right, lucky you."

She leaned down to kiss him, and he was just getting into it when she lifted her head up.

"So how did he get caught?"

It took Walker a second to realize that Lindsey was talking about Red. "Sold a piece to an undercover federal agent."

"Oops. Where were you?"

"I was finishing high school. They wanted me to testify against him, but the lawyer they appointed got me out of it."

She rested her hands on his chest, rested her chin on her hands. "Wait. How did you get out of testifying?"

Walker rolled out from underneath her.

"You're killing me, Walker." When he didn't turn back toward her, she snaked a hand around his waist.

"Are you trying to bribe me with sexual favors?"

"Yes," she said, with absolutely no hesitation.

"If I answer this question, can we be done with the inquisition?"

"We can be done for tonight."

"With the inquisition?"

She smiled at him and kissed his chin. "Yes. Just the inquisition."

Walker sighed and looked up at the ceiling. He really, really liked having sex with Lindsey. But he really, really didn't want to answer her question.

"Hey," she said gently, rubbing a hand across his chest. He thought if he waited long enough, she might let him off the hook.

No such luck.

"I didn't have to testify because I would have incriminated myself."

She wrinkled her brow. "You mean you—"

"I helped him make fake art."

"Oh." She started the rubbing again, then leaned up on her elbow and turned his chin until she was looking into his eyes. "Walker, that's a terrible thing your father made you do."

"Is this going to be pity sex?"

"Hush. I've seen what you do now. You're not painting. You're not faking some historical canvas. That giant metal tree out there? That's your own work. That's all you."

Walker blinked and looked away from her. He knew that. He didn't need Lindsey to tell him that. He couldn't quite explain the squeeze that went from his gut to his throat, but it definitely was not because he'd been waiting a long time for someone who had nothing to gain to see his work for what it really was. Not a way to fake people out, not a way to make money. Just something beautiful.

But he didn't want to think about how much that meant to him, or how much Lindsey was starting to mean to him. So when she crawled over him and asked, "Ready for those sexual favors?" he grunted and flipped her on her back and ended the inquisition.

He loved these people, he really did. They smelled interesting and they gave him good food. But sometimes, he had to run. And when they were busy with each other, doing whatever the heck they were doing, he found his chance to escape for a little while. Getting out of the door was easy, but squeezing through the holes in the fence was a little harder. He had to dig and dig and dig before he could fit through. But then he did fit, and then he was through, and then he started running.

Chapter 16

When Walker woke up, it was quiet.

The sun was streaming through the sheer curtains, which was strange because he didn't have curtains. The sheets smelled floral-y and when he opened his eyes, the sheets looked floral-y, too.

He also smelled coffee.

Three signs that he was not in his own apartment.

When he'd imagined Lindsey's room, which happened with alarming regularity when she first moved in, he'd pictured gauzy curtains and lots of pinks and purples and, for some reason, a lot of fake fur.

Aside from the curtains, he had it totally wrong. Her room was a riot of bold, bright colors—a bright blue bedspread over floral sheets, red curtains made of raw silk, a small area rug with splashes of yellow and orange. But rather than looking like a rainbow threw up, everything somehow tied together. It didn't match at all, and yet, it completely matched. For someone who claimed to have no artistic ability, she had a good eye for color.

Also, there was no hint of fake fur. A sign of good taste.

There also was no hint of real fur, which concerned him because when Booger was quiet, that usually meant Booger was doing something he wasn't supposed to be doing. Walker rolled out of bed and found his jeans, threw them on, and followed his nose to the coffee.

It was in the kitchen, but Lindsey was not. Instead, there was a note. On pink paper.

You looked so cute and peaceful that I didn't want to wake you up, and yes, I said you were cute and peaceful because I knew it would make you all scowly. I'm at work. Help yourself to coffee. Booger (still mad at you for

naming my dog Booger) must have locked himself in your
apt—sorry in advance if he tore anything up. I'll make it
up to you. XXX Lindsey.

His scowly face morphed into a smile. He poured himself some
coffee—black, in a purple mug—and went through the laundry room
to see what havoc Booger hath wrought.

There was no havoc—at least, there was no havoc that hadn't been
wreaked before. There was also no Booger. Walker started walking
through the house, calling the dog, saying "treats" and "walk," knowing those were two things Booger couldn't resist.

Still no Booger. And no Booger when Walker put down the coffee
and went outside, even as he increased the volume on Treats and
Walk. Then he noticed the hole in the fence, and the freshly dug up
grass in front of the hole.

Crap.

He went inside to throw on some more clothes, chugged his coffee, and hopped in his truck to track down his dog.

Lindsey's dog.

Whatever. The lost dog.

"What's gotten into you?" Myron asked as Lindsey turned off the
TV in his room.

"Nothing," she said, throwing the curtains open. "It's a beautiful
day, Mr. Harris. Don't you think you should enjoy it?"

"Why, you know something I don't?"

"I know it's sunny and that television will rot your brain."

"Fine, I'll sit inside and read."

"Or you could go outside and read."

"You trying to get rid of me?"

"No, I'm trying to get you to embrace the day. And to get you out
of here. It's cleaning day."

"Fine. I'll go outside. Tell those guys not to move my stuff!"

Lindsey saluted Myron as he shuffled out the door. She ushered
the cleaning crew in for the scrub-down, and got out of the way as
sheets and disinfectant started flying.

It was a beautiful sunny day, mercifully not too hot. She was well
and truly headed toward her first real autumn. For now, there was a
shed full of outdoor equipment just waiting for some intrepid head

nurse/activity director to pull out and organize. Today, that intrepid person was going to be Lindsey.

As she strode merrily across the lawn, she waved at Mae and Gladys, who were gossiping on a bench under the old oak tree. "You look happy, Miss Lindsey," Mae shouted.

She was happy. The world was bright and clear, there was a bocce ball tournament in her future, the grass was waving, the flowers were blooming. If she wasn't so totally, blissfully happy, she'd have thought she was trapped in a feminine hygiene commercial.

With old people.

And bocce balls.

As she slid the bocce ball set out of the shed, she heard a few shouts behind her. Then the ground shook with a mild thumping, and before she could turn around, she was thrown on the ground, face first.

It only took a second to recognize those giant feet that had her pinned to the gently waving grass. She rolled over and let Booger lick her face before sitting up and looking around.

"Where'd that dog come from?" Mae shouted.

"My house," Lindsey shouted back.

The question was . . . how?

She heard a whistle and turned to see Walker running across the lawn toward her. He was holding a leash. She imagined the leash used to be on the dog.

She should be mad. But Walker looked cute and disheveled in yesterday's clothes, and his messed-up hair reminded her of all of the fun things they did last night to get his hair to look like that, and she just couldn't work up the anger. She took his hand when he offered it, and let him hoist her off of the ground.

"You found the dog," he said.

Lindsey looked down at Booger, who was digging into the grass at their feet. She took the leash from Walker and snapped it onto Booger's collar. "Yup." She handed the leash back to Walker. "How'd he get away from you?"

"Uh . . ."

"Is this the dog we were supposed to go look for?" Myron asked, coming up behind Walker.

"Yeah," Walker said.

"Found him," said Myron.

"What do you mean, the dog you guys were supposed to look for?"

"Uh . . ." said Walker again. "He kind of . . . got out of the yard."

"What? How did he do that?"

"He dug a hole under the fence. Must have done it while we were sleeping."

He lowered his voice on the last word. As if Myron couldn't guess. As if they all couldn't guess, with the way she'd been running around like a happy tampon.

"Oh, you poor baby," she said, kneeling down to squeeze Booger's face. "Why are you trying to escape our love? Don't you know we're your best friends and we're going to love you forever and ever? Oh, you're just too precious. I want to cut off your cute little ears and put them in a sandwich."

"I can't imagine why the dog would run away," Myron muttered.

The lady was talking so funny. He had no idea what she was saying (it wasn't "treats" or "walk," he knew that), but he liked when she talked funny and got close enough so he could lick her face. He liked this place. There was lots of grass and lots of nice-smelling people who petted him a lot. He was going to have to dig out from under the fence more often.

Chapter 17

Basically, the dog was following her to work.

Not that Lindsey minded. Booger was actually really good with the residents—gentle and patient, more or less doing what he was told. The fact that many of the Shady Grove cardigans were now full of dog treats surely had nothing to do with that.

But she couldn't always take the dog to work. It was nice, but it was distracting. Plus, she knew Walker missed him. He hadn't said so—the chance of Walker admitting a weakness was as unlikely as the chance of him willingly telling his secrets. But it wasn't clear who wagged his tail harder when she and Booger came home from work. She was starting to feel insulted.

Walker usually made up for that.

God, he was good in bed. She never would have guessed that a man who was so reserved in real life would be able to open her up the way he did. It had been almost every night since that first time, and if he woke up early enough, every morning, too. She should be exhausted.

She was a little exhausted.

Keeping track of Booger on top of her actual job didn't help. She spoke to the residents about how, for now, Booger was going to be a "sometimes" visitor, not all the time. And since she was pretty sure Walker would sometimes need to leave the house, they had to figure out a way to keep Booger contained.

"We need to fix the fence," she told him over a lazy Saturday cup of coffee.

He raised his eyebrow. "We?"

"Well, you're the landlord, but it's my dog, so, yes. We."

"Do you know how to fix a fence?"

She looked deep into her coffee mug. It contained no answers. "No."

Walker tipped his chair back so he was balancing on two legs. She hoped he tipped over, if that would wipe that self-satisfied smirk off his face. "So, I need to fix the fence."

"Do *you* know how to fix the fence?"

The chair crashed down on all fours. "No."

Since it had been over three minutes since Walker had touched her, Lindsey felt compelled to climb in his lap. That, and the fact that she wanted to preserve her chair legs.

"So . . ." She stroked the hair at the back of his neck.

"So," he said. They looked at each other for a long moment, and Lindsey forgot what the problem with the fence was, again. Something about the dog. And the broken . . . God, he was handsome.

"Linds," he said, brushing a curl behind her ear. "It's pretty clear to me that you already have a plan for the fence, so why don't you just go ahead and tell me."

Oh yeah. The fence. "Well . . . I was thinking."

"Mmm hmm."

"Since we already know a guy who knows how to fix stuff, maybe we could just call him?"

"Who do we know?"

"Jake Burdette."

"Okay, I'll call him."

"Well . . ."

"Let me guess. You already called him."

"I just thought, since you guys sort of knew each other already, that maybe it would be nice for you to work on the project together."

"You don't think he would rather get paid to do it himself?"

"I bought beer."

He looked at her, that little crease forming between his eyebrows. "Lindsey. Are you trying to set me up with Jake?"

She shrugged. "Just as a friend. He's really nice. And he likes to do dude stuff, and you like to do dude stuff, so I thought . . ."

"We could do 'dude stuff' together?"

"Yeah. Plus, Booger really likes him."

"You realize I'm straight, right?"

She slapped his shoulder. "I just want you to have some friends, that's all. You spend so much time alone."

"I like being alone."

She'd hurt his feelings. Real smooth, Lindsey. She knew nothing made Walker more defensive than challenging that Lone Wolf vibe he had going on. She leaned into him, resting her forehead on his. "I know."

He wrapped his arms around her waist. "Quit trying to make me make friends."

"Okay," she said softly.

"I don't need friends."

"I know."

They sat there like that, wrapped up in each other, neither of them believing Walker for a second.

"He's still coming over to fix the fence," she said. "I promised him beer. And that you'd help him."

Walker growled and stood, taking Lindsey with him. He tilted her back, and proceeded to compromise the structural integrity of her kitchen table.

For a man who liked being alone, he sure was good at being with her.

Walker's stomach decided to do a round of somersaults when he saw Jake's truck pull up the driveway.

For god's sake, he was just coming over to install a fence.

This wasn't a damn date.

"Hey, man." Jake climbed out of his truck. "I heard your escape artist got out again."

Walker looked toward the house, where Booger was looking pitifully out of the window at them. "Yeah. Thanks for dropping this off. You didn't have to do that."

"It's no problem." He slapped Walker on the back. Jake seemed to be a bit of a back-slapper. Maybe that was some kind of 'friends' signal.

Or maybe Walker was acting like a virgin on prom night.

He'd had friends before. Jesus, Jake was his friend back in high school. There was no reason to feel pressure.

"You can just unload it here if you want."

Jake tipped his eyebrow up at Walker. "I thought we were putting it up?"

"Well, I don't want to—"

"And Lindsey said she had beer."

"Yeah, it's inside." He led the way inside, then handed Jake a bottle from the fridge.

"Lindsey here?"

"No, she had to go take care of some paperwork."

Jake took a swig. "You know, whenever I try to get Grace to work on a big project at home, she suddenly has to meet with a student or grade papers. It's amazing."

"Oh, I think she really did have paperwork. She's been bringing Booger to work with her, and she said she needed to catch up . . ."

"Relax, man. I'm just joking." He followed Walker and his beer out the front door. "Although I'm not joking about Grace. She hates home reno projects."

"That doesn't bother you? That you do all the work?"

Jake shrugged. "I love that woman, but if you saw her with a hammer, you'd want her to go grade papers, too. It's actually easier if I do all the work. So, are we doing the whole yard, or what?"

Walker walked Jake around the property, showed him where the holes were the worst. Jake declared the fence pretty shoddy—which happened when wood went untreated for twenty-odd years. "Not your fault," he assured Walker. "It was probably not that much better when you bought the place."

"Yeah, but when I bought the house, I didn't have a dog."

You still don't have a dog, he reminded himself, as Booger scratched at the screen on the back door.

Jake shook one of the sturdier-looking fence posts, which sent a ripple down the entire fence. "I don't know, man. I think this whole thing has to go. That's okay, there should be enough." The two men walked to the front of the house again, then to the back of Jake's truck, where he pulled a tarp off the bed.

Walker looked at the fence Jake had salvaged from a finished job where it wasn't needed. It was white. Walker supposed beggars couldn't be choosers, but it looked very . . . wholesome. Did everything Lindsey touch turn to Pollyanna?

"How long is this going to take?" Walker asked. "Not that I have anything better to do—I just want to know."

"That depends," said Jake, hoisting the first piece of fence out of the truck. "How much beer you got?"

WHAT WERE THEY DOING TO HIS YARD.

Chapter 18

Lindsey came home to two sweaty guys sitting on the back porch, drinking beer. She'd hoped to catch them earlier, preferably with their shirts off—with a mental note to apologize to Grace for ogling her very hot fiancé. Alas, Booger's presence at Shady Grove really had put her behind on her work, and she'd spent a very air-conditioned day filling out forms and listening to Mae and Eugene sing old standards at the piano while Myron grumbled in the background.

Jake's chair was tilted back, Walker-style, and his hat was tipped low over his eyes. Walker wasn't wearing a hat, and it looked like he had sunburn on the bridge of his nose.

She wanted to kiss that sunburn. Poor guy.

He reached into the cooler at his feet and handed her a beer. She took it gratefully, but, finding no bottle opener, stood there lamely, the sweet relief of a post-work beer taunting her with her lack of simple tools.

Walker came to her rescue, though, and held out his hand. She gave him the beer and watched, appalled, as he opened it with his teeth.

"You're going to break your teeth!" She wasn't scolding. She was just giving her opinion as a medical professional.

Walker just handed back the beer. She smiled at him. He shook his head, but she saw him hide a smile behind his own bottle.

She sat down on the top step and admired their properly fenced-in yard. "Looks great," she told the guys. "I didn't know you were going to do the front, too." The white picket fencing ran all the way around the house, so the front and back became one giant yard. "How do you like it?" she asked Booger, who was lounging sleepily on Walker's feet.

"He's been running laps for an hour or two," said Jake. "I never saw a dog so happy to have a fence."

"No wonder he's pooped. Aren't you, boy?" She scooped Booger into her arms and let him snuffle around her neck. "Are you guys hungry? I'll cook." She was tired, but she hadn't just set up a fence around an entire yard. She still felt like she owed them.

"Sounds good, but I gotta get home to Grace. She's making lasagna."

Lindsey's stomach growled. Lasagna sounded good. Did she have the stuff to make lasagna?

"I thought her lasagna was terrible?" Walker asked.

"It is, but once she burns it, we'll order a pizza." Jake clinked his beer against Walker's raised bottle.

"You could just order the pizza to begin with. Save her the trouble," Lindsey said, feeling the need to stand up for the sisterhood.

Jake shrugged. "She likes to try. And who knows? Maybe this lasagna will be amazing. You gotta be open to the possibility, you know?"

"I like you, Jake," Lindsey told him.

"Of course you do. He's a goddamn Pollyanna," Walker mumbled.

"What was that?" Lindsey asked, even though she heard him perfectly well. Spending so much time with Myron had greatly improved her mumble-deciphering skills.

Walker just smiled at her, then drained his beer. "It's a good thing you're so cute, you know," she told him. Jake snorted.

"Well, I hate to leave this cozy scene," he said, plonking the chair legs down and standing up. "But I'm afraid if I hang around too long, Lindsey's going to come up with more work for me to do."

"Take me with you," Walker pleaded. *Ha ha,* thought Lindsey. Some landlord.

"See you later, man," said Jake. Walker nodded, and Lindsey tried not to get too excited that maybe he and Walker were going to hang out on their own, and not just because she was making them perform manual labor together.

"See you, Jake," she said. "Thank you so much. I'll bring you brownies."

"Bring them next week. Grace is going to see her sister for the weekend. Maybe I'll actually get to eat one or two this time."

"How about I bring you some tomorrow *and* next week?"

"Lindsey," Jake said with a very serious look on his face, "I love you."

She laughed. "Good-bye, Jake."

" 'Bye. Oh, Grace said to call her. Girl stuff."

She went inside when Jake's truck pulled away, if only to hide the ridiculous smile she was sporting. Girl stuff. She had a girlfriend now, and Walker had a boyfriend now. If she and Walker were a couple, they would have a couple-friend.

She stopped in the kitchen doorway.

That was how it started. First the couple-friends, then all the friends that were part of a couple, then it was nothing but double dates and dinner parties and soon she would be just one part of Lindsey-and-Walker.

Good thing they weren't a couple.

"Are you really cooking?"

She jumped when she heard Walker's voice right behind her. Then she blushed, but not because she was feeling guilty for trying to convince herself that she was not part of a couple with the man she was sleeping with practically every night.

She was not actually sure why she was blushing.

Probably just the beer.

"Sure," she said. "I can't promise lasagna." She rooted around in the fridge—definitely not lasagna. "How about pasta and vegetables?"

"You got any meat in there?"

She opened the freezer. "Chicken breast?"

"Dammit, woman, I just did some hard labor. I need real meat."

She checked the fridge again. "Sliced turkey?"

"Pathetic. Good thing I have steak."

"If you have steak, why are you digging around in my kitchen for dinner?"

"Because if it comes from your kitchen, I don't have to cook it."

She shook her head and shoved him, which was maybe just a little bit of an excuse to feel those rock-hard abs. "Let's grill. You make the steak, I'll grill the vegetables, and I'll come up with something amazing for dessert."

"How amazing?"

"I won't know until you leave me alone so I can figure it out."

So he did, but not before he smacked her on the ass on his way out the door.

Good thing he's so cute, dammit.

Walker said a silent thank you to Myron and his constant need for diversion. If he hadn't insisted they try the new butcher in Hollow Bend, Walker would have nothing in his fridge. As it was, he had steak. Steak, a really old bottle of ketchup, and some mystery rice. Fortunately, the butcher also had some marinade, so he set the meat to soak it up, then went outside to turn the grill on.

On his way out the door, he heard his phone beeping. Three missed calls from a number he didn't recognize. Then, as if the number was waiting for him to be nearby, the phone rang again, the strange number blinking at him. "Hello?" he said as he navigated the screen door.

"Walker?"

And that just about put him off steak for good.

"Red. You're not calling collect?"

"Is that any way to talk to your old man?"

It probably wasn't, so Walker kept his mouth shut.

"You there, son?"

He hated it when Red called him "son." It just didn't sound right. Even though, technically, biologically, it was. "Yeah."

"You know what today is?"

Walker wracked his brain. Red's birthday was on Christmas Eve—another in a long line of injustices he'd had to suffer—and Walker's wasn't until the fall. He really couldn't think of another reason why his father would be calling.

"I'm out, son. Parole board said I was good enough to reenter society."

"Great." Walker thought about the mail from the Ohio correctional facility, sitting unopened in a drawer in his kitchen.

"That's it? No, congratulations for your old man? No, say, What can I do for you, Dad, now that you've paid your debt to society?"

Walker didn't say anything.

"I don't know what you're mad about," Red continued. "You're not completely blameless in all this, you know."

Walker felt a rage bubble build in his gut. He took a deep breath before it could explode out of his mouth and into the phone. He had sworn he wouldn't let his dad get to him, not ever again.

But damn him. Red hadn't changed at all. Nothing was his fault; nothing he did ever caused any damage.

"I've paid my debt to society now. Can we move on, son?"

If you quit calling me son, Walker thought.

He heard Lindsey talking to him before he saw her, pushing her screen door open with her butt. She was still talking when she saw him on the phone, but she stopped and made an "oops . . . sorry" face. He waved off her apology and took the excuse she gave him to end the call.

"Okay, well, thanks for calling." And he hung up.

"Sorry about that," she said. "I didn't hear you on the phone."

"It's okay." He started the grill, then went back inside for the steak. His phone rang again, but he silenced it, then shut it down. When he came back out, Lindsey was in the garden, pulling at toma-toes. "Do these look ripe to you?" she called, but he pretended not to hear her.

Damn him. Damn Red Smith and his guilt trips. And damn me for falling for it, Walker said to himself.

"Walker? You okay?"

This was not what he needed. Dinner with Lindsey would mean an inquisition and he had already told her more about his dad than he wanted to. Red didn't deserve the air Walker would use to tell the story, and Red didn't deserve the space he took up in Lindsey's brain, where she was no doubt trying to figure out a way to make it all okay. But as she walked up the stairs, holding a not-very-ripe-looking tomato, with that look of gentle concern on her face, he knew he couldn't sit down with her and not spill his soul out at her feet.

He needed that soul. He needed to keep it close, like he always did. "Uh . . . I lost my appetite, that's all."

"Too much sun?" she asked, but the look on her face told him that she didn't even believe herself.

"Yeah. I think I'm just going to . . ." He didn't even finish the sen-tence, just headed for the garage. His work was the only place he'd be able to completely lose himself, to keep Red far from his mind. Which was ironic, since Red's forgery complicated Walker's feelings about his own work. But even Red's duplicity and scapegoating couldn't take away the power Walker felt when he was in the grip of his artistic drive.

He didn't turn around, just shut the garage door quietly behind him.

So much for dinner.

Lindsey watched Walker's retreating back, noting the tension in his posture. Lost his appetite. Sure. Well, if he wanted to play the starving artist—literally—that was none of her concern.

Even though his phone was sitting right there next to the grill, and it would be the easiest thing in the world to just swipe the screen to see who the last caller was . . .

No. Sneaking into his phone was just as bad as sneaking into his studio. Worse, somehow. She was just going to have to sit on her hands while she ate dinner.

Lindsey found she no longer had an appetite for steak, either. She took the plate of meat into Walker's kitchen, wrapped it up, and stuck it in the fridge. Then she went back into her kitchen to mope. It hadn't been her plan, but she'd been looking forward to dinner with Walker. She was just going to have to get used to the fact that she was sleeping with a moody, temperamental artist who needed his space before she'd be able to grill him about his problems.

She'd also lost her appetite for cooking, and definitely had no appetite for eating alone. She thought about calling Grace, but then remembered Jake and the lasagna. Then she thought about Mary Beth, but she was probably doing something with Will and the baby. God, all of these couple friends. She finally called Helen, whom she didn't know very well—she was single, surely she wouldn't have any plans on a Saturday night.

Helen answered the phone from the coffee shop downtown, where her date was apparently not going to show. Good, thought Lindsey, then immediately felt appropriately guilty because, well, it wasn't very nice to be glad a friend was stood up. To be fair, Helen didn't sound all that disappointed. So Lindsey quickly changed into a cute sundress with a matching sweater and headed out to meet Helen for margaritas and, if they felt like it, dinner.

If she was gonna leave me, the least she could do is leave me in the garage with the big guy. Geez.

Chapter 19

Lindsey fumbled with her key before she finally got it right side up and then actually into the lock. She turned to wave good-bye to Helen and her friend, Henry, who had come to rescue them when they lost track of the number of margaritas each had consumed. Pitchers had probably not been the best idea. Well, one pitcher had been a fine idea. But then that one got empty somehow, and they had to get a new one.

Fortunately, Henry had been on call in case Helen needed rescuing from her bad date. When he texted her to see whether she was having fun or being ax murdered, her response was so margarita-garbled that Henry rushed right over. He was cute, and a history professor, and he and Helen started talking about some papers that had been donated to the Pembroke Library and Lindsey's eyes started to glaze over until she realized that these two spoke the same language, and surely they would speak the same language in bed.

The sudden stunned silence made her realize she'd said that out loud.

Oops. Well, what was the worst that could happen? Helen and Henry could reveal non-mutual romantic feelings and their relationship could be ruined. Or . . . or they could realize that the mad, passionate love each carried like a secret torch was the same mad passionate love carried in the heart of the other. And they would name their first baby Lindsey.

Or, she could just not drink so much.

The problem with margaritas, in addition to severely impeding her driving, was that they amped her up. Maybe it was the sugar, or some magic in the tequila, but when she drank margaritas, if there wasn't a dance party nearby, Lindsey was apt to create her own. She needed to find her iPod.

Instead, she found Booger staring mournfully at the back door. "Poor baby," she said, and let him out.

He made a beeline for the fence, and while she watched him sniff and huff like a crazy beast, she couldn't help but notice the lights on in the garage.

Old habits die hard, she chided herself.

She and Walker weren't in a fight. He just needed some space. That was hours ago. Surely hours was enough space. And he had a radio in there, she was sure of it. Iron Maiden radio. They could have a dance party, and then they could do her second-favorite thing to do when she drank tequila.

This would call for seduction. If he was in a funk, the only way to get him out would be some slinky lingerie. He hadn't seen any of her slinky lingerie. She knew it cheered her up. Had to work on him too.

Propping the screen door open so Booger could come back in when he was done being Booger, Lindsey skipped up the stairs and dug around in the back of her pajama drawer for the robe and teddy set she'd bought when she broke up with Brad. It was a deep burgundy with lace around the edges, very low cut and very short and very silky against her skin.

The effect was somewhat ruined by her flip-flops, but she wasn't going into that garage barefoot. Besides, if Walker was smart, he wouldn't be looking at her feet.

She walked out into the yard and stood at the open garage door, listening. He was being pretty quiet. Maybe he was concentrating. Maybe he was napping. "Walker?" she called softly, then stepped inside. She saw a movement in the corner, near the big doors of the garage. "Ha. You can't hide from me, you know." She slid the robe off of her shoulders and listened to it whisper against the concrete. "Walker," she cooed.

But when she rounded the table, the man crouching down at the roots of Walker's tree was not Walker at all. He was big and bald and had a short beard and suddenly Lindsey didn't feel so drunk anymore.

Instead, she screamed.

* * *

Walker woke up to the scream.

He had been really, really asleep, and it took him a second to process what the sound actually was. Was it even real?

Then the scream came again, followed by Booger barking like crazy.

Lindsey.

He shot out of bed and out the back door. He saw the lights in the garage and all he could picture was Lindsey in a freak air stapler accident. He skidded through the open door.

Lindsey was standing at the base of his tree, screaming at it.

And she was wearing . . . what the hell was she wearing?

He almost said, damn the danger. He wanted to fling her over his shoulder and lock her inside until he could get a really good look at the short, strappy, shiny thing she was wearing. And he might have, had he not caught a movement from the ground.

Someone else was there.

Which explained why Lindsey was wielding a lead pipe.

God, she looked hot.

He took a step forward, and she must have seen him because she turned and opened her mouth again, but this scream died out into a whimper. She was scared, and that drove him into action. In one step, he was in front of her and her pipe, and reaching for whoever was skulking around his garage.

He saw the back of a head, but didn't take in more than that before he pulled the guy up by the neck of his shirt and shoved him back to the ground.

The guy turned onto his back and put his hands up. "Walker!" he yelled.

The voice stopped him cold.

"Red."

Goddammit. His father was here.

Chapter 20

This was Walker's father?

Lindsey wasn't sure what she was expecting, exactly. Not someone quite so . . . hard.

According to Walker, he was a con man and an art forger, but maybe she'd seen too many movies because she was expecting a warm and charming guy. She wasn't quite prepared for the thick, wiry muscles. He was short, and he really didn't look like Walker at all, except for maybe in the nose and eyes. Walker's eyes had been wary and closed off when she'd first met him, but now she could read them like a book. His dad's were the same steel gray, but when he smiled, his eyes didn't look happy at all.

And he did smile—another difference between Walker and his father. Red Smith smiled a lot, and asked a lot of questions about Walker and how he'd been, and asked what Lindsey did and how she liked living here and he hoped his son was treating her well. Despite his scary appearance, he acted very friendly, like it was no big deal that he had broken into his son's studio and was now just sitting around making small talk.

Of course, she wasn't one to judge others for breaking into Walker's studio.

But the eyes really bugged her. Cold. That was what they were. Walker could be grumpy and private, but when he smiled, Lindsey knew he meant it. Heck, when he smiled, she felt it zap down through her core.

Red's smile made her squirm in an entirely different, entirely unpleasant way.

But he was Walker's father. And he hadn't actually done anything wrong in this case—at least, nothing that Lindsey hadn't also done, and Walker seemed to like her okay. Maybe Red looked that way because he was just out of prison. Maybe he just needed some time to get used to civilization again. Her opinion was probably clouded by Walker's own dislike. She wasn't going to give the guy a kidney, but she also wasn't going to let Walker kick him out into the cold night.

Which was exactly what Walker wanted to do.

"You don't just 'swing by,' Red."

Lindsey noticed that Walker didn't call him "Dad." Clearly, the two were not close. But she didn't miss the hurt flinch through Red's face every time Walker did it.

"I told you I was getting out."

They were sitting around Walker's kitchen table, all very cozy and domestic. Lindsey had changed into sweatpants, and helped herself to Walker's coffee pot. Red drank the coffee like it was going out of style—best coffee he'd had in ten years, he told her. She tried not to be flattered.

Walker just stared hard at his father, even when Red looked away and admired the house.

"Quite a spot you've got here," Red told him. "You've done well."

"All on my own," Walker said quickly.

Red threw up his hands. "Hey, I never said otherwise. I always knew you were the real deal, son."

"Don't call me that," Walker muttered, then took a sip of his coffee. Lindsey put a hand on his knee and squeezed. Walker was doing a good job of being mostly polite, but she could see Red was pushing his buttons. She didn't really know what those buttons were, but Walker's muscles were tightly coiled under her hand, and she wanted to stand up and wrap her arms around him.

That might interfere with the tough-guy act he was putting on for his dad, so she stayed seated.

Lindsey let the silence linger between the two men. She had tried to fill it with small talk, but every time she engaged Red in conversation—that was another way he was different from his son, he actually knew how to make small talk—Walker got kind of a pre-transformation Hulk look about him. So she tried to keep her mouth shut. As a result, she was drinking a lot of coffee.

"What are you doing here, Red?" Walker asked again, despite the fact that Red had answered that question more than once. The first answer, "I thought you'd be glad to see me," was clearly bull. It was pretty obvious that Red was not surprised by the cold reception he was getting from his son. Hurt, maybe, but not surprised. The second answer, "Just stopping by on my way out of prison," was ridiculous.

Red sighed, as if Walker had finally worn him down and he was bracing himself to reveal the truth. Very dramatic, that sigh.

Lindsey gripped her mug tightly, trying not to die of curiosity.

"I got nothing, kid," Red began. "I been inside for ten years. Got no money, got nowhere to go. I hitched a ride here—you know how hard it is to hitch a ride to Bugtussle, Kentucky?"

"Real sorry I couldn't live somewhere more convenient for you," said Walker, oozing sarcasm.

"Look, I know we have our differences." Walker snorted, but Red continued. "I know you think I did you wrong growing up, and maybe I did. I was just trying to teach you how the world works. I know I'm not the world's greatest father"—Walker snorted again— "but I did my best. I taught you how to survive, didn't I? And look how you turned out. I'm proud of you, son."

"Are you seriously taking credit for my life?" Walker's back muscles trembled under Lindsey's hand, even as she rubbed small circles with her thumb. He took a deep breath. "One more time. What do you want?"

"Ah, son, don't be so hard on your old man. It's hard for me to ask for help."

"No." Lindsey flinched at the coldness in Walker's voice.

"Just for a few days. Just until I can get my feet under me."

"No," Walker repeated.

The two men stared each other down, and Lindsey felt the residual chill coming off them.

This was ridiculous. He was Walker's father.

She cleared her throat.

Neither of them looked her way.

"Red," she said, tentatively. She still couldn't believe "Red" was actually his first name. "I'm sure you understand why Walker has mixed feelings about you visiting."

"They're not mixed at all," Walker said, still staring down Red.

"But," Lindsey continued, "I understand that you are going through a . . . transition period."

Now both men looked at her. Red looked grateful. Walker looked like he wanted to dump his coffee on her head.

"I'm not suggesting he move in," she told Walker. "Maybe just for a few nights."

Walker's mouth opened, then closed. The muscles in his jaw clenched so hard, she thought his teeth were going to break.

"But Red," Lindsey said, turning to the older man, "you have to respect Walker's space. He's worked hard for his success, and he's under a tight deadline." Walker raised his eyebrow at her. She hurried on—she was no good at lying, and even if this was just a little fib, she didn't want to dwell on it. "So you need to give him room to work. And you need to stay out of the studio unless you're invited in. You can use these few days to find a job and a new place to live, but if Walker doesn't want to talk to you, you have to respect that, okay?"

Red smiled, but not at Lindsey. "You got a real sweet woman here, you know that?"

Walker clenched his jaw.

"Just a few days, son, I promise. I'll keep out of your way until I find my feet, and then I'll be out of your hair for good."

"Promise?" Walker asked tightly.

"Yeah, I promise."

"You can stay, Red. One week. I know your promises don't mean shit, but mine do. Today is Sunday. You're out of here next Sunday, no excuses. Got it?"

"Got it," Red said, a little sadly, Lindsey thought. "Thank you, son."

"And quit calling me that."

I don't like the smell of this guy. I gotta keep an eye on him.

Chapter 21

"I meant it, son. You got a real sweet woman out there."

Walker ignored his father, and instead focused on a mental inventory of the valuables in his apartment. He had the small fireproof box that contained his social security card and bank documents, and a copy of his contract with the Madison Kelly Gallery. A contract he needed to work on fulfilling, although not with any of the urgency Lindsey suggested earlier.

Lindsey. He stopped being mad at her as soon as she softly kissed him and thanked him for taking in his dad. She had no idea what Red was like, but Walker knew what Lindsey was like, and if there was any hope at all of a situation having a bright side, she would find it. He didn't hold out much hope that Red was going to turn into a model citizen, but she was right. He was just out of prison; he had nowhere to go. And even though Walker's first instinct was to tell his dad that he didn't owe him a thing—and, in fact, that had been exactly what Walker had done—Lindsey was right. A little human kindness wouldn't kill him.

He still wasn't leaving anything valuable in his apartment.

Lindsey brought over an extra toothbrush and found a clean set of towels for Red. He gave her that damn charming smile of his, but she didn't hang around to hear more of his sad story. Instead, she told Walker that she'd see him in a minute, and left the two men alone in Walker's bedroom.

Walker didn't know what she was expecting—a sudden father and son heart-to-heart, probably. Well, Walker might have been willing to give up his bed for a few nights, but that was about it.

"And a sweet house," Red said, apparently unaware that Walker was giving him the silent treatment. "You got it all, don't you, son?

The dog and the yard and the sweet woman. You done good for yourself."

No thanks to you, Walker wanted to snap back at him. The only thing that stopped him was that he didn't want to give Red the pleasure. Because if Walker fought him, Red could say that his own son, his only flesh and blood, had kicked him when he was down, and that was why he wasn't able to turn his life around. Instead, Walker just walked downstairs and outside, made sure his studio door was locked and padlocked, then headed back in through the open laundry room door. He whistled for Booger, who looked at him from the top of the stairs, then went back into Walker's bedroom.

Great. His dad was even taking his dog.

He ran into Lindsey pulling sheets out of the dryer. "I think Booger is guarding Red," she told him.

"What does he need guarding from?"

"No, I mean I think Booger's keeping an eye on him."

Smart dog, thought Walker.

"You want to help me make the bed?"

Sure, he could help her make the bed.

He took the bundle of sheets from her and she led the way up to the bedroom. She tossed the pillows onto the floor. Walker fished the fitted sheet out of the pile and handed her one end.

They stood across from each other, snapping the sheets tight and pulling the quilt up. It looked cozy.

"Uh," said Walker, like a genius, "do you have another blanket?"

"Why? It's not that cold." She looked puzzled. Walker took that as a good sign.

"Wait," she said, not so puzzled. "You don't have to sleep on the couch."

"I didn't want to assume—"

"Unless you want to sleep on the couch."

"Hell no."

She smiled at him. "Good."

"That couch is way too ugly to be comfortable."

"Hmph." She walked around the bed toward the dresser. "I could make you test it out."

He grabbed her around her waist and pulled her close. "No way."

She laughed and swatted his shoulder. "Come on. I have to get up early tomorrow."

Well, so much for that.

She took out a pair of pajamas—nothing at all like the maroon thing she'd been wearing earlier, dammit—and went into the bathroom. Walker sat down to pull off his shoes. They were really going to sleep together. Just sleep. That would be a first for them. He thought he should probably go next door and get some pajamas. Did he even have any pajamas?

But then Lindsey came out of the bathroom, looking adorable and clean and sexy. He recognized her little shorts as one of his favorites, and her tank top was doing all kinds of great things for him. Her face was scrubbed clean and as she got closer, he smelled her minty fresh breath.

She nudged him off the bed and pulled back the quilt. She climbed in and he thought, forget it. No pajamas. He tore off his shirt, stepped out of his jeans, and climbed in right next to her. They snuggled down and he put his arms around her. She sighed and put her head on his chest. He rubbed her back.

It was all very cozy.

He had a dog, a white picket fence, and now he was sleeping with his sweet woman. Just sleeping.

"So. Your dad."

He should have known they wouldn't just be sleeping. This was Lindsey. Of course they'd be talking.

"My father."

"He seems . . . nice."

"Yup, he seems that way."

"But he's not so nice?"

"He's fine, as long as you don't count on him for anything."

"Or try to buy art from him."

Walker hissed out a laugh.

"Does he look different? After ten years in prison, I mean."

Walker shrugged. "More muscles. Less hair."

She was quiet for a while, and Walker braced himself for whatever she was going to ask next.

Instead, she said, "You did the right thing, letting him stay."

"Yeah, well, apparently I'm a good person now."

She squeezed around his ribs.

"So you didn't know he was getting out?" she asked.

"Yeah, I knew."

"You seemed surprised to see him."

"Wishful thinking. Or maybe I was surprised to see him sneaking into my garage, ogling my—" His what? His girlfriend? His sweet woman?

She leaned up on her elbow and smiled at him. "What?" he asked her.

"I didn't say anything!" But she was still hovering over him, smiling down.

"Something funny . . ."

"What?" she asked.

"What happened to that slinky thing you were wearing?"

"I don't know. It didn't seem appropriate."

"No, probably not." He sighed.

"Are you complaining about my pajamas?"

"No! I would never . . ."

"Or are you just trying to change the subject?"

"No! I like these." He brushed the strap of her tank top off her shoulder and placed a kiss there. He felt her heartbeat speed up against his chest and she leaned heavily into him. "Sorry," he said, sliding her strap back in place. "You have to get up early tomorrow."

She scrunched up her nose in a pout. But then her face softened, and she brushed some hair off his forehead. "Thank you for letting him stay." She rested her head on his chest again. "I know you didn't do it for him."

How did she do that? Cut through whatever crap he was telling himself before he even knew it was crap? She was right. He didn't do it for his dad. He wasn't sure why he did it, not until Lindsey thanked him.

He'd let his father stay for her.

He wanted to believe what she believed, that people defaulted to good and that everyone deserved, if not a second chance, then at least common decency. He didn't believe it, but wanted to, so he'd given Red his bed because he knew that's what Lindsey would've done, and he knew it would make her happy.

There was no way she was getting to sleep now.

She wasn't sure why she said it. She knew it was true, but she planned on keeping it to herself. But then he kissed her shoulder and that one little brush of his lips had her primed and ready for all kinds of fun that would make it hard to get out of bed in the morning—and then he stopped. It wasn't a sense of revenge that made her speak the truth. She wanted him, not because he was hot (although he was) and not because he knew how to make her feel good (although he did), but because he was Walker and he did that nice thing for her even though it meant doing something nice for his dad and, at that moment, she really loved him for it.

But she didn't want to say that. So she said, "Thank you," and then she was airborne, lifted on top of Walker, his hands digging under her tank top, his mouth rough on hers. She pulled her shirt over her head and was just getting down to the business of reveling in the feel of his strong, bare chest against hers, when she was thrown off balance again. This time Walker was on top of her, and his hands were everywhere—on her breasts, in her shorts, down her legs. And everywhere his hands went, his mouth followed, biting and licking and not at all the gentle Walker she'd experienced that night on the kitchen table, but she liked this one, too. She might like this one even more, she thought as his teeth closed around her nipple and his hand squeezed her butt. She gasped and groaned and bucked up into him. Everything was happening at once and too fast and she couldn't keep up, though not for lack of trying.

"Hold still," he whispered, and she almost laughed at the impossibility of that request. Instead, she just squeaked out "I can't!" as his clever fingers worked their way around to the front of her. So he pulled her arms up above her head and gave her the crookedest, wickedest smile she'd ever seen and that almost had her losing it right there. But then he took one of his hands and touched her again, then guided himself into her, and she gasped and tried to keep her hips still but whatever, she was a bad listener. He twined his hands in hers, but pulled them down so they were next to her ears. He propped himself up on his elbows, their fingers intertwined, and he started moving.

It didn't take much for her. One, maybe two—she was completely and happily incapable of counting at that moment. She just shouted and arched and Walker was right there with her, squeezing the life out of her hands while he shuddered and growled.

She heard Booger howl from next door, and then she thought she might die because if the dog had heard, then Red had probably heard.

"Do you think he heard us?" she asked when she had enough breath back to form words and make them come out of her mouth.

"No," Walker gasped, then flopped down next to her. She decided she would just believe him. He put his arm over his eyes, and she did the same.

She thought she might have died for a second there.

But she didn't. She just mildly had her mind blown. Her ears were kind of ringing. *All those nerve endings freaking out,* she thought.

"Hey." When he pulled her arm down, she saw him leaning over her. "Are you okay?"

"Mmpsh," she said, meaning, "nerve endings" and "dead."

"Did I hurt you?"

You killed me, she thought. But it didn't hurt. She shook her head, but it didn't wipe the worried look off his face. "No," she assured him, putting a hand on his cheek. She pulled him down for a kiss, and lifted a knee to cradle him close to her. "No," she whispered against his lips. *But if you keep looking at me like that, you will.*

Chapter 22

As Walker approached the laundry room door, he heard Booger's mad scratching and picked up the pace. He really didn't want to replace another door.

Although that might make Lindsey happy. Give him a reason to have a date with Jake again.

He shook his head. The woman was strange, but he liked her. She tried to do what was best for him. He wasn't going to start bro-ing down with the whole county, but Jake was an all-right guy and Walker was glad to have made a friend.

So what if he had to be tricked into it by his . . . by his Lindsey.

He opened the door and Booger bolted through, running a lap around Lindsey's apartment. "She's at work, buddy," Walker told the dog. "I know. I wanted her to stay home, too."

"You talking to the dog?"

And that was why he wanted Lindsey to stay home. It was a little bit easier to face his father when Lindsey was there. He felt less like he might murder the guy.

But Walker had promised Lindsey that he would give Red a chance, and Walker was not the kind of guy who took promises lightly, even if those promises were tricked out of him by the pressure of an amazing set of breasts against his arm.

"Sleep all right?" Walker asked.

Red looked surprised. "Fine, yeah. Once the dog stopped growling at me."

Walker patted Booger on the head.

"Breakfast?" Walker asked.

"You cooking?"

"Sure."

"You still make those egg waffle sandwiches? Remember those?"

Walker remembered. Scrambled eggs with ketchup sandwiched between two frozen waffles. He made those for dinner the first time when he was about twelve because he was pissed that Red hadn't bought any groceries and wouldn't let them order takeout. If Red wouldn't get him real food, his adolescent brain reasoned, he would show him by eating something totally disgusting.

Walker knew now that it was because Red had no money, but at the time, it seemed like Red just wanted to piss him off. So Walker wanted to piss him off right back. Instead, Red had laughed, like Walker was some kind of culinary genius, and ate two of them.

They actually weren't bad, the waffle-egg sandwiches, especially when he added bacon.

This must be the bonding portion of the visit, Walker thought. Reminisce about the good old times when Red was a shitty father and Walker learned never to trust anyone.

"I don't have any waffles," he told Red. Even if he did, he wasn't going to make Red a special sandwich, dammit.

"How about we go out somewhere. My treat."

"I thought you didn't have any money, Red?"

"I got enough to buy my son breakfast. Just make it somewhere cheap." Red laughed his damn head off and slapped Walker on the back.

Great. The bonding portion of the visit was just beginning.

Thursdays were Walker's day with Myron. He sometimes spent other days with him, too, but every Thursday they had a standing lunch date.

Lindsey pretended she wasn't watching for him at the door of Shady Grove.

So did Myron.

Walker had been simmering a low-burning rage since his father had come to stay. He was ornery and short-tempered, and was always trying to walk away from her rather than have a conversation. It was just like when she first moved in.

She did not reminisce about that period fondly.

In Walker's defense, he didn't snap at her, and she could see him trying not to snap at his father. This meant that Walker spent a lot of time in the garage. He would work until late at night, then come crawl into bed with her. Sometimes he'd just hold her, sometimes she'd insist she was awake, so he better get to smoochin'.

No matter how gentle (or not gentle) he was at night, though, in the morning he was back to his silent, grumpy self.

Myron, for all his flaws, had some kind of magical power, as if his own grumpiness somehow neutralized Walker's. That was the one time she'd seen Walker smile since they discovered Red in the garage—when he was here, visiting Myron.

"What's he like?" Myron asked from his seat by the sunny window.

"What's who like?"

"The pope. Who do you think? Walker's dad."

"Didn't you meet him? Back when you were teaching?"

Myron snorted. "Red wasn't exactly a get-involved kind of parent."

Lindsey sat down in the chair next to Myron. It was sunny, and the day was quiet. She could take a break. Or, if she kept talking to Myron, she could call it an assessment.

"I'm worried about Walker," Lindsey said, totally failing to assess Myron. "He's not handling this well."

"Handling what? What's the guy doing here, anyway?"

"He just got out of prison, Myron. He didn't have anywhere else to go."

Myron waved her concerns away. Lindsey knew she had talked Walker into letting his father stay, and she still thought it was the right thing to do.

She, apparently, was the only one who thought so.

"Well, speak of the devil," Myron muttered. And just like that, Walker came through the door, followed by Red.

Oh, this should be fun, she thought.

"Hiya, sweetie," said Red, using his brand-new, super-fun nickname for her. "Cute scrubs."

Lindsey made a mental note to burn these scrubs.

"Hey, Red," she said politely. "Hey, Walker. We were beginning to think you wouldn't show." She tried to communicate empathy in her gaze.

"You got a problem with your face, Lindsey?" Myron asked.

Lindsey sighed. So much for meaningful looks.

"You must be Myron," Red said, holding his hand out for a shake. Myron looked at it. "You didn't bring the dog?" he asked Walker.

This is going great. Lunch will be fun, she thought.

"So, where are you guys off to today?" she asked in a voice that sounded forced, even to herself.

"Actually, I was gonna let the boys have their time," Red told her.

"Big of you," muttered Myron.

"I thought I'd see if you needed any help around here. You know, to pay you back for putting me up."

"Oh," said Lindsey, surprised. She looked at Walker, but his face did not give her any clue about what she should do with Red's sudden generosity. "Okay, sure. Um . . ." What could she have the ex-con help her with?

"I can do some landscaping if you need it. Or help out in the kitchen . . ."

"Well . . ."

"Or just hang out with people. I miss hanging out with people. If you've got some supplies, I could teach a painting lesson."

"I bet you could," muttered the ever-helpful Myron.

"Gosh, that's . . ." She looked desperately at Walker, who shrugged like that idea was probably fine.

She did a quick mental inventory of the art supplies. Gladys and Mae came out from the lunchroom and watched the little group curiously.

"What do you say, ladies?" Red asked them. "Should we paint some happy little trees?"

If she set Red up in the art room, she could keep an eye on him while simultaneously getting him out of Walker's hair for a while. Plus, Red was obviously a good painter. After all, some of his forgeries worked, she thought. And he would only be here for a few more days. How much damage could he do?

"Okay, that would be great. I'll get you set up." With a quick glance back at Walker, she led his father to the art room, trailed by some very curious senior citizens.

Chapter 23

Walker pounded through the front door.

Red was sitting innocently in the easy chair, reading a magazine. He was even wearing reading glasses. The picture of innocence and civic responsibility.

Then Walker noticed his duffle bag, packed and zipped by the edge of the couch.

"What did you do, Red?"

"I don't know what you mean," he replied, flipping the pages.

"You going somewhere?" Walker kicked the duffle.

"My week is almost up. Thought I'd get a head start, is all."

Walker narrowed his eyes at his father. "I'll ask one more time . . ."

"I didn't do anything! I told you, I've changed. I'm not the guy I was before I went in."

"Yeah, I know. You've had ten years to think about your crimes."

"You can get sarcastic about it, but it's true."

"You suddenly realized that what you did was wrong?"

Red stood up and threw the magazine onto the floor. He turned away from Walker and into the kitchen.

Of course he hadn't realized what he did was wrong. Red Smith would never admit he was wrong.

"I did a lot of things I shouldn't have, but I was just trying to provide for you, son. The government says I paid for my crimes. When is that going to be enough for you? I was just trying to make a life for us."

"Some life. Was that why I ended up in foster care? Were you so busy out providing for me that I wore shoes with holes in them?"

"Oh, poor Walker! Like you're the only one who's struggled. And look at you now! I must not have done too bad if my poor, neglected son became a world-renowned artist."

"That has nothing to do with you."

"Doesn't it? Who taught you about art, huh, kid? Who's the one who showed you how light and dark play off each other? Who taught you how to capture movement and sound in a goddamn picture?"

"You taught me how to copy other people's masterpieces. That's not art, Red. That's forgery."

"All art is forgery, Walker. Wake up."

"Oh, big existential talk from the con man who lost his touch."

"That's right. That's me, a washed-up old loser who didn't have a father to support his talent. I shared my gifts with you, son, and what did I get for it? Ten years behind bars, where I had the creativity sapped out of me, staring at those damn cinderblock walls. You might think I'm a con man, but I was just playing the game using whatever I could. And now—" Red's voice broke, and Walker actually felt a little sorry for the guy. He might have been a con man, but at least he'd had something. Now he was just a con man without a con.

That sympathy quickly disappeared as Walker thought about how much time Red had been spending at Shady Grove.

"Red. What are you really doing here?"

"I told you. I need to get back on my feet. Don't worry, though, I'm out of the art game."

"What game are you in?"

Red straightened so he was toe to toe with Walker. "I'm in the game of life, son. And you can sit here in your pretty house with your pretty white fence and your pretty dog and your pretty girl, but some of us don't have it that easy. Some of us've gotta take what we can, or we're out in the dirt with nothing. Don't you dare judge me for that."

Walker stepped back and crossed over into Lindsey's apartment. He came back a minute later with his little fireproof box. He pulled out a check and started writing.

"Take this," he said, handing the check to Red.

"Oh, son," Red said, sounding suddenly contrite and grateful. "I can't—"

"It's not a gift. I'm buying you off. Take this, and never come back here again. Whatever information you took from those people at Shady Grove, lose it. Lose it, or I'm calling the cops on you."

Red stared hard at the check.

"So you'll rat out your old man again?"

"That's right. I'll rat you out, but not because I'm bitter that you were a crappy father. And not because your world view is so screwed up that you think everyone is out to get you, when really you're just too lazy to figure out how to do things right. I'll do it because what you're doing is illegal, and it's wrong. Those people worked hard for that money. And even if they hadn't, even if they were born with a goddamn silver spoon in their mouths, it doesn't matter. It's not your money, Red. You're not entitled to it just because you think you're smarter, or because you can take it."

"I am smarter. It's not my fault people are too stupid to hold on to what's theirs."

"You're right, Red. Nothing is your fault."

Red tried to skirt past Walker, but he held firm, made himself a wall between Red and whatever he wanted to take that he didn't deserve. As far as Walker was concerned, Red was done taking.

He must've gotten the message, because he finished shoving his clothes into his duffle, and yanked the zipper so hard it broke off.

Walker guessed that was his fault now, too.

Red looked down at the check. "This is real generous of you, son, but I got no way to get anywhere."

Walker didn't hesitate. He grabbed the key ring out of his pocket, pulled the keys for his truck off, and tossed them at Red's feet.

The older man started to say something, but Walker just turned on his heel and went upstairs. He sat down on his bed, his spine straight. He listened until he heard the truck pull away, then dropped his head into his hands.

When Lindsey got home from work, she noticed Walker's truck was gone. She called out as she went inside. When no one answered, she figured Red was gone, too. Maybe they were off having a fun male bonding trip.

Or maybe Walker was burying the body.

Not funny, she thought. *Walker hasn't had a murderous gleam in his eye since the first night Red showed up.* But Red did need to get a move on, his wonderful art lessons notwithstanding.

She'd done some research on how ex-cons can enter the workforce. It wasn't going to be easy. Red would need someone willing to give him a chance, and it probably wasn't going to be his dream job, at least not at first. But if he could get his foot in the door and prove himself, Lindsey was sure he could get back on his feet.

That's why she'd spoken to Ned Grubb. Red had been so great with the seniors, encouraging and instructing, and all without any preparation. He was a natural teacher, and if he could channel his talents for good, he could make a real difference in the world.

Ned was willing to hire him to help Glen in the kitchen on a trial basis. It wasn't glamorous, but it was a start. Red could keep teaching classes, and eventually, he would build up enough work experience that he would have an easier time finding a job. Preferably, a better job in a new city.

Not that she didn't like Red. It was just that . . . well, she didn't like him. She hated to admit it, especially since she seemed to be spending so much time telling Walker to keep an open heart. But Red was Walker's father; Walker was never going to escape that connection, so he might as well make the best of it. Lindsey couldn't shake the creepy feeling she got from him, though. She couldn't explain it. He was perfectly nice to her—more than nice, he was generous and helpful and told her that she was good for his son. She had no evidence that he was anything but reformed.

She chalked the creepy feeling up to her own prejudice, a prejudice she didn't know she had. He'd been a criminal. But he paid his debt, and she wouldn't let his past dictate how she felt about him.

She tried. She really tried.

She tried for Walker's sake. But if she was really honest with herself, she would rather Red was gone. And since the main obstacle to his leaving was his lack of gainful employment, Lindsey was pretty pleased with herself for managing to find a solution to the problem that would suit both Red and Walker.

She would miss sharing her space with Walker. Not that it was official—all of his clothes were still in his apartment, and he basically just slept in her bed. (Well, slept and did other stuff—hooray for other stuff.) She liked waking up with him. She realized she was getting dangerously close to having a relationship, but she didn't mind. It didn't count if she didn't have to give up any closet space for him.

Poor Walker. Kicked out of his own place and forced to live apart from his clean boxers. She would make it up to him. She thought about the lingerie set, and how disappointed he'd been that he hadn't gotten to see it up close. Maybe she'd send Red out to the movies so Walker could get a real good look at it. Maybe she'd spring for a double feature.

As she walked through the kitchen, she noticed that the light was on in the garage. Maybe they could get a do-over on the last time she tried to seduce Walker.

But if Walker was in the studio, where was Walker's truck? He was pretty adamant about not letting Red drive it since his driver's license had expired while he was in prison. And where was the dog?

Then, as if she'd conjured him, the garage door opened and Booger came galumphing out, followed by Walker. He was backlit by the overhead lights, and it made him look angelic until the door closed behind him and he was just regular old Walker again.

Good thing she liked regular old Walker.

She met him on the steps to the back porch, her curiosity trumping her desire to seduce, or at least re-prioritizing her desire to seduce. She still had plans for that lingerie.

"Hey," she called. He looked up at her and gave her a tight smile.

At least it was a smile.

"Get some work done?"

He nodded.

Okay then.

She leaned down to snuffle Booger, who was bouncing madly at her feet. At least the dog was glad to see her.

"Where's Red?" she asked, squinting up at Walker.

"Gone," he said, and shoved past her. Snuffling as she was, she lost her balance and landed attractively on her butt, legs rising in a slow-motion, failed attempt at balance. "Sorry," Walker muttered, and grabbed a hand to right her. "You okay?" he asked.

She raised her eyebrow at him. "If I wasn't, would you start acting like a human being?"

He ran his hand through his hair. Lindsey recognized that as Walker's I'm-frustrated-but-not-at-you gesture. She'd become very familiar with that gesture this week. As soon as it was near enough, she put her hand on his forearm. That was her You-can-tell-me-about-it gesture.

Walker didn't take the bait, though, and turned away from her toward his back door.

"Hey," she said. "Is Red okay?"

"Yup," Walker said. She followed him inside.

"Did you let him borrow the truck?"

Walker didn't respond. Something was definitely wrong, and Walker had put up those old walls again. She hated those damn walls.

"Walker!"

He whirled around to face her so quickly that she had to take a step back. "He's gone, okay? I gave him money, I gave him my truck, and he's gone."

"What?"

Walker didn't repeat himself. That was fine. Lindsey had heard the words, she just couldn't make sense of them. "What do you mean, you gave him the truck?"

"I mean he needed a way to get out of town, so I gave it to him."

"Why did he need a way to get out? Did something happen?"

Walker ran that frustrated hand through his hair again. "Not yet."

"Not yet? What does that mean?"

"It doesn't mean anything, okay? He's gone, that's all you need to worry about."

Lindsey tried to put out her listening hand, but Walker backed away.

"Stop it, Lindsey. Just drop it."

"Drop it? But—"

"Dammit, Lindsey! It's none of your damn business. Just leave it alone! In fact, just leave me alone."

"What?" she asked softly. She was beginning to sound like a real idiot.

"You heard me. Stay out of my business. Stay out of my life. None of this would have happened if you had just kept your mouth shut."

She recoiled, but Walker wasn't done. "I should've just kicked Red out the second I saw him, but you had to stick your nose in it and tell me what was best for me. Well, you were wrong. He's not my father, not in any way that matters. He's not reformed. He's not secretly a good person."

"What did he do?"

"He didn't do anything, not yet. But he could have. He would have, and you know why he would have? Because you let him. You let him stay, and you showed him kindness. But Red doesn't see it as kindness, he sees it as weakness."

"And so you saved me from the big bad man, is that it?"

"God, Lindsey, you are so naïve, you know that? You've got your head up in some goddamn rainbow clouds. Wake up, Lindsey. My father is an asshole. No amount of magical thinking is going to change that."

Lindsey stared at the man she thought she knew. She thought his gruff exterior hid a soft, gooey inside. And maybe it did, but if it did, she still hadn't hit it. "I guess you're right. You're a lot more like him than I thought."

She waited a second to see if he wanted the last word, to see if he would argue with her, prove her wrong about him. She was wrong about Red, fine, but she didn't have to be wrong about Walker.

But when she turned to go, he let her.

Booger sat on the back porch, looking at two identical closed doors. He looked back and forth, left and right, waiting for someone to come out and tell him which one was his. But nobody did, so after a while, he went back to his old spot under the porch and fell asleep.

Chapter 24

Walker tried to convince himself that it was nice getting to sleep in his own bed again. It probably would have been nicer if he'd actually gotten to sleep. It had been a long time since his insomnia had hit. Months.

He didn't miss it.

It didn't help that he could trace his last bout with insomnia to right before he started sleeping with Lindsey, and that she was just next door, and that he really should talk to her anyway because he definitely owed her an apology.

Instead, he spent a productive night staring dumbly at the ceiling. The only thing that broke up the monotony was the occasional howl from Booger.

At least yesterday was over. He'd given Red an hour's head start, then called Ned Grubb over at Shady Grove. Walker had never been a great talker, but he thought he'd done a pretty good job convincing the owner that there was a possibility that the personal information of some of the residents had been compromised, without telling him how he knew. Well, he thought he'd been convincing until Will Brakefield showed up at his front door.

Since Red hadn't actually done anything—yet—there were no charges to press. And Walker didn't have proof that Red had actually taken anyone's data, and it was entirely possible that he wouldn't, since identity theft was a different game from art forgery. But Walker had seen that old chip on Red's shoulder when he left, and Walker knew that when Red thought he deserved something, he took it. There was no reason to think he might not at least try.

Walker half hoped he would try. With extra safeguards in place,

Red would surely get caught, and then he'd be out of Walker's hair for another ten years. Or more.

But maybe Lindsey was right. Maybe Red had changed. Maybe he was only *thinking* of defrauding senior citizens out of their retirement savings, but wasn't actually going to go through with it.

That was some Lindsey-level magical thinking, there. The most Walker could hope for was that Red wouldn't try to steal anything, at least not for a while. By then passwords would be changed and alerts would be posted, and Red would realize the jig was up and that would be that. He could hope that Red would be satisfied taking the lion's share of Walker's savings and his only mode of transportation, and that would be it, at least for a while.

Now all Walker had to do was repair the damage Red had done.

Who was he kidding? It was he who'd done all the damage. Red might have been the wheel that set it in motion, but Red didn't put a gun to Walker's head and tell him to act like a total dick to Lindsey. The things Walker said to her—totally uncalled for. So what if she saw the good in people? So what if that good wasn't there? How had that hurt anyone?

Now that it was morning, what he really needed to do was go to Shady Grove and talk to Lindsey in person. But, of course, he had no way of getting there. He'd just have to wait until she got home. The groveling he was building up to was not something that could be accomplished on the phone.

So he locked himself in the garage, and he worked.

Lindsey was an idiot.

Ned said she was being too hard on herself, but Lindsey thought she wasn't being hard enough. She'd almost hired a known fraudster to work with a vulnerable population. She knew that senior citizens were particularly at risk for identity theft. She knew that, but she'd planned to hire Red anyway because she wanted him to be a good person.

Walker was right. She was naïve. She was a fool. The fact that Walker had stopped her from being an accessory to a crime didn't help.

"You got a burr under your tail?" Myron was standing at the door to her office.

"What?"

"It's an expression. You look pissed off."

She sighed and waved him in.

"I am. At myself, mostly."

"Because you let Red Smith dupe you?"

"Gosh, Myron, don't try to spare my feelings."

"Eh, you caught it in time."

"I didn't catch anything," she reminded him.

"That's right. Walker did. He's not anything like his father, you know."

Lindsey looked up, surprised. "I know that."

"He's a good boy. He just needs to learn to trust himself."

Great, now they were going to have a heart-to-heart about Walker. What were the chances that Myron wouldn't notice her crying?

"Hey, now, none of that."

Pretty slim, clearly.

"I'm okay," she said as Myron shuffled around her desk. He pulled a tissue out of the box and handed it to her.

"What did that boy do?"

Lindsey was surprised by the anger in Myron's voice. She reminded herself that she needed to keep it professional.

"Nothing, really. He's just . . . he's very upset about what happened, and so am I. I'll be fine. Really. I promise."

But she wasn't fine. She cried the whole way home, and she cried when she took herself to bed early. She was still sniffling when she heard Walker knock softly on her door, but she wasn't ready to talk to him yet, not like this.

She dozed for a bit, and when she woke up, she was sensible.

There was no reason to cry. She had nothing to cry over. She'd been dumped before. She'd ended much longer relationships than the one she had with Walker. She didn't even want to be in a relationship. She wanted to do things differently. She used to have boyfriends. She didn't want one now.

Totally different.

Dammit, her eyes were still leaking.

It was too confusing. She didn't want Walker, especially if he didn't want her. She should be grateful to him. He'd prevented her from slipping into her old pattern of pairing up with someone, and not having time for herself. He had actually done her a favor.

The wind slammed rain against her window. At least if she was sad and miserable, this would be the perfect weather for her.

But she was fine.

She hadn't even bothered changing out of her scrubs before getting into bed, and now she was up at 2 AM listening to the rain, but that was just because she was fine.

She was going to need another minute or two before she could admit that Walker had broken her heart.

Her phone beeped, and she dug it out from under her pillow. Her ridiculous, traitorous heart thought for a minute that it might be Walker, calling to apologize and admit he was an idiot. She was ready to talk to him, now that she was sensible.

But it was the number for Shady Grove. She sat up, immediately alert. A phone call from a nursing home at 2 AM could not be good news.

"Lindsey? I'm so sorry to wake you." Hope sounded frantic and breathless. "Mr. Harris is missing. He's not over there, is he?"

"What?" Lindsey jumped out of bed and grabbed her socks and sneakers.

"I know he's friends with Walker. He was up reading a few hours ago, but when I did my last round, his bed was empty. We looked everywhere. He's not here."

"Did you check the sun room?"

"Yes, and the kitchen and all of the other residents' rooms. Lindsey, he's not here."

"He can't have left. Wouldn't the alarm have gone off?" She threw a fleece on over her T-shirt, then grabbed her raincoat out of the closet. Flashlight. She had a flashlight somewhere. Kitchen drawer.

"It must have shorted out when we lost power earlier . . ."

"Don't we have a backup? Okay, no, obviously not. Listen. I'm on my way in. Call the police, tell them everything you remember. When was the last time you saw him? What was he wearing? They're going to want to know all of that."

"Lindsey, I'm so sorry. I checked on him. I swear he was in his room—"

"Hope, listen to me. Hope. Stop. Listen. Deep breath. Call the police. Answer their questions. Stay there and wait for them, okay? I'll be there in a few minutes."

"Oh, god, Lindsey, what if—"

"Hope, no. I'll see you soon, and we'll find him."

She hung up on Hope, and slammed the door behind her.

Walker was an idiot.

But breaking up with Lindsey was the smart thing to do. It never would have worked out. She was Mother Teresa, he was a con man's son. Even if he did give them a chance, sooner or later she would realize they were not meant to be together, and she'd go. And he wouldn't be able to blame her. But he could cut a little of that pain off at the pass.

He'd made the right decision.

Being right sucked.

He was startled out of his pity party by a knock on the door.

"Walker?"

Lindsey.

He thought about hiding in his room. She'd ignored his knock earlier, so now it was his turn.

Right, because she was so crazy in love with him that she needed to pound on his door in the middle of the night to declare her undying love.

Not that he wanted that.

And why wouldn't she just pound on the laundry room door?

While he tried to figure out what she was doing there, she continued to pound on the door and shout for him. There was only one way to find out what she wanted. He pulled the door open, and his heart stopped.

Something was wrong.

She was pale and disheveled, her hair spilling out from the hood of her raincoat.

"Is Myron here?"

"What?"

"Is Myron here? Just tell me."

"No, of course not, it's the middle of the night."

She cursed under her breath, and he knew it was really serious. "Lindsey, what's wrong? Come in, let's—"

"No, I have to find him. He's missing."

"What? When?"

"Tonight. I don't know how long ago. A few hours, maybe. Is there anywhere in town that he would go? Favorite spots? Where did you take him when you guys went out?"

Walker started a mental inventory: the Duck Puddle, the Daily Drip, the high school. There were so many. "Give me your keys. I'll drive."

They found him by the side of the road, where the shoulder sank down into a low ditch. It was dark, and Myron was barely conscious. They would have walked right by him if Booger hadn't suddenly gone nuts, running down the road as Walker chased him, then back and forth between him and what Walker soon discovered was his friend, his face twisted in pain. Walker cursed the time they'd taken to meet up at Shady Grove first, even though all that accomplished was Lindsey comforting a freaking-out Hope while Booger, who had jumped in the car back at the house, jumped out again, running loose inside, then tearing out the door and down the road.

Walker shouted. He slid down next to Myron, checked his breathing.

"My ankle," Myron groaned, and Walker saw it, twisted at a strange angle in his slippers.

He tried to think. Booger was barking his head off and Walker couldn't think. He should lift Myron up. He could carry him back to Shady Grove. He wasn't that heavy. It wasn't that far. But as he put his arms under Myron's back, the old man shouted out in pain, then cursed at Walker.

"No! Don't move him." Suddenly Lindsey was by his side, her pants covered in mud where she had slid down next to him. "Where does it hurt, Mr. Harris?"

"His ankle," said Walker. She thrust her flashlight into his hands. "Hold this on him. Do you have your phone?" Walker nodded. "Can you hold the flashlight and call 911?" Walker nodded, then did as she asked, propping the flashlight under his chin while he dug his phone out and dialed.

"Mr. Harris?"

"Dammit, call me Myron!"

Walker laughed with relief. If Myron was cursing, he would live.

"Myron, I need you to be as still as you can." While she ordered him around, she was pulling off her raincoat, laying it over him. "What happened? What were you doing out here?" Booger ran circles around them, stopping to lick Myron's head and whimper in concern.

"I just slipped, that's all. My damn ankle," he said, ignoring her second question.

"Does anything else hurt? Hands? Arms? Head?" She took the flashlight from Walker and shined the light quickly in Myron's eyes.

"Get that out of my face! And get that dog off me!"

"How many fingers am I holding up?"

"How many am I holding up?" he grunted, then gestured in a very impolite manner.

"Twenty minutes or so," Walker told Lindsey.

"Okay. God, that's a long time."

"There's a fire in the next county."

"I'd like to get him out of the mud. I don't want him getting hypothermia."

Walker moved to get under Myron again. He would have carried him to the hospital, but Lindsey stopped him. "Wait."

She ran into the woods and came back with two short, thick branches. "Take these for a second." She tore off her sweatshirt, then took the branches back. "I'm going to make a splint, Myron. It will hurt for a second, but this will stabilize your ankle so we can move you, okay?"

Myron yelled in response as Lindsey gingerly lifted his foot and ran the sweatshirt underneath it. She wrapped the branches against his ankle, then tied it tightly. "Okay, can you lift him?" she asked Walker.

Finally feeling useful, Walker worked his hands under Myron's slim body. Lindsey held gently onto the ankle and Walker stood. "Careful," she murmured. Once he got to the road, Walker wanted to run up the driveway to the nursing home. He could see the lobby lights in the distance, then a pair of headlights. Booger stood next to him, barking at the Shady Grove van.

"Good boy," Lindsey said, and flagged it down. Glen had been called in on the search, and he pulled up next to them, hopped out and helped Walker load Myron onto the bench seat. Lindsey took Walker's phone from him and gently pushed him into the passenger seat, and Booger jumped in next to him and took position facing away from the windshield.

Lindsey climbed in next to Myron and Walker heard her calling to re-route the ambulance to Shady Grove instead of to a ditch by the side of the road. He heard Myron groan and turned around to see Lindsey clasping his hand, her T-shirt caked with mud, Booger's head on Myron's lap. Walker turned around to face the lights of the nursing home so she wouldn't see the tears welling in his eyes.

"He's in good hands."

Walker looked like he wanted to throw a chair or bend a pipe, he was so tense. She put her hand on his shoulder and felt the heat radiating off him. It felt kind of good. She was wet and cold.

"They'll just be a few more minutes, then they'll want to take him to the hospital for X-rays and to make sure he's okay."

"It's just a broken leg, right? Nothing more?"

She sat down next to him and took his hand. "I think so. But they have to make sure his blood pressure stays okay, and he was out there for a little while, so they'll need to make sure he doesn't have hypothermia. In my experience, they usually keep seniors overnight, even if it's just for observation."

"But he'll be okay?" She heard the crack in his voice and she wanted to wrap her arms around him, but he was squeezing the life out of her hand and she didn't think he would let her go.

"Do you want to go with him?"

"Yes," he answered before she even finished the question.

"I'll call his daughter."

"Oh, right. She'll want to come down." He ran a frustrated hand through his hair. "I was supposed to take care of him."

"Walker." Still holding onto his hand, she squatted in front of him.

"He was coming to see me. He knew I was upset about . . ." He trailed off, and Lindsey didn't let herself finish Walker's thought. Because if Myron had run off because she and Walker were fighting, this was her fault, too.

Walker cleared his throat. "My father, and everything. But I told him I was going to see him in the morning. I was going to bike over and meet him for breakfast. Why couldn't he wait?"

"I don't know. But, Walker, Myron made the decision to sneak out on his own. It was a stupid decision, but it was his. And I think he was confused. But there was absolutely nothing you could have done to prevent him from doing that." That sounded pretty convincing. She hoped it worked on Walker, because it sure wasn't working on her. "That was our job."

He shook his head.

"And you found him. You saved him," she reminded him.

"Booger found him. You saved him. I just stood there."

"Okay, that's it. I'm not going to entertain this pity party any more. I'm wet, I'm cold, and I have to write up a report about this. Go to the hospital. I'll stop by and check on him. I'll bring some of his stuff. I'll call his daughter."

Visiting hours were long over, but Walker couldn't bring himself to leave. He also couldn't bring himself to get comfortable in the waiting room chairs. Good thing he was used to not sleeping.

Myron was sleeping. He had taken some pretty serious pain medicine and didn't recognize Walker, but when he talked to his daughter on the phone, he knew her. He was talking crazy loopy to her, but he knew her.

She would be there in the morning. Walker offered her his room. He would sleep on the couch.

Good thing he was used to not sleeping.

"Hey."

He turned around and blinked. He hadn't realized how bleary his eyes had gotten. He thought it was just the TV being weird. But, no. There was fuzzy Lindsey, and then, as she stepped forward, clearer Lindsey. She was still wearing her muddy sweats, but she had an oversized UK sweatshirt on. Right. Because she'd destroyed her clothes saving Myron. She looked pale.

"Hey," he said to the woman who had saved his best friend's life.

"You gonna stay here all night?" she asked, taking a seat on the bench next to him.

"I hadn't really thought about it."

"The nurse said he's sleeping."

"Drugs."

"And that he's doing really well. Crabby, but well."

"I know."

"There's nothing else you can do tonight."

He sighed. "I know." There was nothing he could do before, either.

"Walker." He looked up at her as she stood. "Let's go home."

He let her take his hand and lead him out of the hospital.

* * *

Lindsey still had adrenaline pumping through her system. First from working on Myron, then from keeping her cool talking to Shady Grove's lawyer, who chewed her out for calling Myron's daughter before calling him.

The only thing that stopped her from punching him in his lawyer face was the look on Ned's face. He was just as shocked and disgusted as she was.

She was going to go home, take a shower, and pass out. But she was still kind of hyper in a way that she hadn't been since she'd first started nursing, when every emergency was her own personal responsibility. She'd felt that the life or death responsibility was hers alone, and not that of the team alongside her. In the ensuing years, she learned to separate herself from the job. She still cared, and probably more than was healthy, but she was able to put a sort of nurse-distance between her and her patients, especially when she was treating them.

But Myron wasn't just a patient. He wasn't just a resident of Shady Grove. He was her friend, and he was Walker's friend.

She didn't like to think that Walker would get him in the break-up, but she supposed Walker had first dibs on Myron. She looked at Walker, pale and tired in the passenger seat.

And just like that, she got her adrenaline crash.

It started with just a few tears. But then she saw Walker turn and she couldn't help the sob that escaped her throat, and it got so bad that she had to pull over and just rest her head on the steering wheel and let it all out.

"Linds." Walker pulled up the parking brake, then pulled her arm until she leaned into him and sobbed onto his shirt. He was much more comfortable than the steering wheel.

That did nothing to help her sobbing situation.

"Hey, are you okay? You're shaking."

"Ad-ad-adrenaline crash," she stuttered.

"What do you need? Do we need to go back to the hospital?"

She shook her head. "Just give me a mi-mi-minute."

He kept his arms around her as a minute turned into ten. At some point he turned the heat up, full blast, and the hot air and the hot Walker had her relaxing a little.

"I'm okay," she said, sitting up and wiping her nose attractively on her borrowed sweatshirt.

"Let me drive," he said, and before she could protest, he was out his door and had hers opened.

She was only going to half protest anyway.

When they got home, he walked her into her apartment. She needed a shower, and she needed to sleep. And probably to cry for another fifteen minutes or so. But before she could do any of that, Walker was in front of her, leading her into the bathroom, turning on the shower, pulling off her clothes.

"Let me take care of you," he said as she started to protest. "Please."

She looked into his eyes, and she understood what this meant to him. It was a gift. A gift of gratitude, a gift of recompense. She was too tired to think of what it meant beyond Walker handing her into the shower. She shivered as the hot water sluiced down her cold skin.

"Where are you going?" she asked when he let go of her hand.

"I'm going to make you something hot to drink."

She shook her head and held out her hand to him.

"Lindsey, I should—"

She cut him off with another shake of her head.

He peeled off his clothes and joined her.

Lindsey was so grateful for Walker's strength and warmth that she turned off the thinking part of her brain, the part that told her that this was a bad idea, that Walker had made it clear he was done with her, that she shouldn't get used to the idea of turning to him for comfort.

Instead, when he stepped into the shower, she stepped into him. He wrapped his arms around her and that, combined with the hot water streaming down her back, got her shivering again.

"Are you still cold?" He cupped her face in his hands, his eyes bright with concern.

She shook her head. His eyes turned dark. She pulled his hips closer to hers and he bent his face down and kissed her.

It was hard and frantic, like the first time they kissed, but there was something deeper behind it. She knew him now, knew what he liked, knew that if she bit his lower lip he would growl and pull her closer. As he tightened his hold, her feet left the ground so she wrapped her legs around his waist. He grunted and she stopped kissing him, but instead of complaining, he kissed a hot trail down her neck and pushed her up against the shower wall. He moved his arms under her butt and lifted her higher, and then his mouth was on her breast and the feeling of his tongue and the hot water almost melted her. But then his grip slipped and she slammed her foot against the rim of the tub and he let her down gently.

When her feet were safely on the ground, he held her face and kissed her again and she leaned into him, feeling him hot and hard against her stomach. But then he was gone, turning the water off, and throwing the curtain back. He rubbed a towel over his head, then roughly over hers, and before she could tell him that, hey, she was not even close to done, he had pulled her close again, then parted her thighs and lifted her wet body against his.

"Hold on," he said, and she did and he kissed her and walked her into the bedroom, dropping her on the bed so Booger jumped off in surprise.

The dog whined and ran out of the room, probably to sit on the couch he was not supposed to sit on. Lindsey didn't care because Walker was on top of her, his mouth on her breast again, and she was clutching his shoulders and pulling him closer and he moved up to her mouth and she let out a gasp because suddenly he was inside her, filling her, making her whole, and then he moved and she came apart. He groaned his release into her mouth and collapsed, pulling her in close as he rolled to his side. She ran her hand up his chest and held him tight as their breathing slowed and their heartbeats lined up and before she could ask him to stay, she was asleep.

He didn't want to sleep on the bed anyway. Even though it would probably be warm. Tonight, he was pooped, even more than the time Walker took him to the dog park and he ran and ran and ran until he thought his legs would fall off, and then another dog came and he ran and ran some more. That was a great day.

But today was a different kind of tired. They were both so freaked out and there was nothing he could do to make them feel better, but at least they let him stay close by. But then he had figured it out. When they got to the nursing home and he smelled Myron's stuff, but not Myron. He would find him. His nose was strong. Even outside with the wind blowing all kinds of great smells around him, he didn't stop in his mission. And he found Myron, and they petted him and dried him off and now he was tired.

He nosed his way under the blanket. This was a treat. Normally

Lindsey told him to get off the couch once or twice before she finally let him sit under the blankets with her. But tonight he had the couch and the blanket all to himself and he stretched out under the blanket and before he knew it, he was chasing rabbits in his dreams.

When she woke up in the morning, Walker was gone.

Chapter 25

Myron was eating it up.

Not that he loved being in a wheelchair, but he couldn't hide his pleasure at the blankets rearranged on his lap, the homemade cookies shared with him, the solicitous attention paid to his well-being. Even Eugene was being nice to him.

Lindsey was glad to have so many people keeping an eye on Myron. It had been an exhausting morning. Myron was released first thing, and Glen had gone in the van to pick him and his daughter up. As soon as Myron returned, he was effusive with apology and gratitude, which was so unlike him that Lindsey almost sent him back to the hospital. Then Darlene hugged her and cried and clung to her and said she was so sorry and so thankful to her, and it was nice to be appreciated, but Lindsey was still feeling a little fragile this morning and the sight of the other woman's tears threatened to break down the small barrier keeping her own back.

Now Darlene was making arrangements to stay through the weekend, and Myron was enjoying Eugene reading to him, even though it was Jesse Stuart.

Lindsey was locking Myron's pain pills up and adding a note to his chart about the additions to his medication. So she didn't know that anyone else had come in until she heard the clicking of nails on the tile and then Booger was alternating between sniffing her shoes and jumping up to try to lick her face.

"Hey—" And then there was Walker in the doorway, empty leash in hand. "Hi," he said, as he reached for Booger's collar and reattached it. "Sorry about that."

"That's okay," she said, ushering them out of the medicine closet and shutting the door behind them. "Hey, handsome." She knelt down to scratch Booger behind his ears, and he immediately flopped down for a belly rub. She laughed, and tried not to look at Walker's boots still standing there.

"I thought we'd check on Myron. Darlene called to tell me he was released this morning."

"He'll be glad to see you."

Walker nodded, then rubbed the back of his neck. *Uh-oh,* Lindsey thought. "About last night—" he started.

Nope. She was still rocking that fragile-barrier thing. She couldn't handle another "You're too naïve" from Walker.

"Sorry, I have to check on—" She didn't even finish, just brushed past him, past the common room, and started her rounds about three minutes after she'd finished the last round.

Booger whined as Lindsey rushed down the hall, but Walker held tightly to the leash. "I know how you feel," he said, because he was now the kind of guy who spoke out loud to his dog. "Come on, let's go find Myron."

"Son," said Myron as he accepted Walker's help into bed. "Do you remember when we first met?"

"Hey, don't get romantic on me, Myron."

"You started shop class in the middle of the year," Myron said, ignoring him. "You were a skinny kid, like a string bean, and you needed a damn hair cut."

So much for the romance. "Yeah."

"Everyone was halfway through making their napkin holders. Remember?"

"Yup."

"And I thought, well, I can have this kid sit on his hands for another few weeks, or I can try to get him caught up. Do you remember that?"

"Yeah." Myron's accident must have jogged some kind of memory-lane impulse he'd never had before.

"And you did. I showed you the scroll saw and the air hammer and you caught right on. Of course, now I know why you were so good with tools, but I was impressed then."

Walker still had that pineapple-shaped napkin holder. He used it to hold his mail. Probably not what his dad had in mind when he taught Walker how to make frames and stretchers for his canvases.

"It doesn't matter what your dad taught you, though. You always caught on quick."

Walker leaned over to fluff Myron's pillow, but the old man batted him away.

"I knew from the start that you were a smart kid. That you'd do something great."

Walker couldn't help it; his pride puffed up just a little.

"I want to ask you something, kid," Myron went on, gesturing Walker closer. He looked tired, so Walker leaned in.

And Myron slapped him upside his head.

"Ow!"

"What's the matter with you, son?"

"What's the matter with *you*?" Walker asked, rubbing his ear.

"That's what I was coming to do last night. That's why I ended up in a ditch by the side of the road. Because you're not smart at all. You're a damned idiot!"

"Whoa, calm down."

"Don't tell me to calm down. Not when there's a beautiful, kind woman who is probably not as smart as I thought, because she's in love with an idiot like you."

"Hey—"

"But then, you're not as smart as I thought either, so you two idiots belong together."

"Myron—"

"Don't you 'Myron' me. I see the way you watch her. I know you got some funny ideas in your head about what's good for you, but I'm telling you, you're wrong. *She* is good for you."

"I know she is."

"Then what are you doing? Why is she still moping around like you kicked her puppy?"

"She is?"

"Yes, she is."

"Huh."

"Yeah. Kinda hard to see with your head up your ass, isn't it?"

Walker smiled. But then he stopped. "Myron, I can't. I can't do that to her."

"Can't do what to her? Seems like you did it pretty good before."

"She shouldn't settle for someone like me."

"Someone like you? What does that mean?"

"I mean, she's got this great family, and she's so . . . optimistic. She doesn't see the world the same way I do."

"I think we've already established that your view is messed up."

"You know where I come from. My dad . . ."

"Red is a scoundrel and a liar, but he's not you. You spent all this time trying to separate yourself from him—and you've done it. You've proven that you are not him, not that you needed to. Anyone with half a brain can see that."

"I know, but—"

"So if you've separated yourself from your old man, what does it matter what he does? How does that affect you anymore?"

"It doesn't, it's just that—"

"Cut the crap, son. You're just scared, is all."

Walker suddenly found the toes of his boots very interesting.

"Hey," Myron said, and he looked up. "I know you think you don't deserve her. But I know you, kid. I know what kind of man you are. And you're exactly what she deserves." Myron held his eyes. "Don't be a fool, son."

Chapter 26

Walker's front door opened as Lindsey climbed up the front porch steps.

"Oh, uh."

She saw Jake Burdette start to back into the house. He, apparently, was stopped by Will Brakefield, who was right behind him, followed by Junk Store Josh.

"Hi, guys." Great. Walker was having friends over. She should have friends over. Friends wouldn't mind if she wore sweatpants, would they?

"Hey, hi, Lindsey." Will was acting awfully fidgety.

"Everything okay in there?"

"Yes! Everything is great, Lindsey!"

"Great. Why are you shouting, Jake?"

"No reason!" Jake shouted. "Gotta go!"

Then the three of them zoomed past her shoulder and were down the walkway and at their trucks before she could say " 'Bye, weirdos."

She shook her head—men were strange. Then she let herself into her apartment and headed straight for the sweatpants.

As usual, Booger had other ideas. Lindsey was surprised to see him inside her apartment. She figured if Walker was home, he would have commandeered the dog, like he usually did. God, he didn't even want her dog anymore.

Whatever they had, it was well and truly over.

"At least I've got you, buddy." Booger tilted his head at her. "Yeah, I know. I don't make any sense to me, either." She led him to the back door.

She was just going to let him out to do his business, but something in the yard caught her attention. Something big. Something . . .

It was Walker's tree. At least, she thought it was Walker's tree. She recognized the shape of the trunk and the movement of the branches. She had spent enough time looking at it while he was building it.

But something about it was not Walker's tree. It was . . . more.

She knew he was going to eventually cover the frame with something that looked like bark, but she had no idea it would look like this. Even the internet snooping she'd done when she first moved in had not prepared her for this.

The tree looked real. But at the same time, it was obvious that it was made of metal. The detail in the trunk and the . . . it had leaves now. Hundreds and hundreds of individual leaves attached to the branches. They moved with the wind and she thought they were made of paper or fabric, but as she got up close, she saw that they were all metal. Thin, detailed, individual leaves. No two were the same, and they seemed to be made out of different materials. How had he found time for that?

And the trunk. She had expected the trunk to look like, well, a dead tree trunk. She could see the detail in individual pieces of bark, solid and rough under her fingers. But he had draped something around the trunk that looked like a soft band of fabric. She ran her fingers over the band—it was smooth and cool. It ran around and around the tree until it blended up and became part of the branches.

She stood close to the trunk and looked up and just completely lost her breath. The sun shone through the leaves, catching the light and making it dance. It looked like what she imagined music would look like. When she'd seen the tree in progress, she was in awe, but this. *This is overwhelming,* she thought as she blinked back tears. *This is so much. This is Walker.*

"Do you like it?"

She squeaked and quickly rubbed her eyes. Not quickly enough, because when she turned around, Walker was standing close enough to wipe the tears off her cheeks.

"Yeah." She gave a watery laugh. "Yeah, I like it. God, Walker. It's amazing. I had no idea it would—" She flapped her hands uselessly. She had no idea it would anything. "How did you . . ." There were so many questions swirling around in her head that her tongue couldn't land on just one.

Walker helped her out. "The leaves are different kinds of scrap metal. So is this," he said, running a hand over the fabric-like wrap.

"How did you get it out here?"

"Will and Jake. And Josh."

"Ah. That explains why I ran into them at the door."

"And that explains why Jake was shouting like a maniac."

"Was this a surprise? For me?"

He nodded.

"What about the gallery?"

He shrugged. "The gallery will borrow it."

"Walker, I can't let you do that. You need to sell this. Your dad took—"

"I've got it worked out. Don't worry."

She looked back at the tree, taking it all in. "How are we going to get it back into the garage?"

"We're not."

"It can't stay out here. It'll be ruined."

"No, it's supposed to be outside. That's the idea I got from you."

"From me?"

"Yeah. The leaves are all different kinds of metal. They're supposed to rust, and when they do, they'll change color." He ran his fingers over one of the leaves and she could picture it dripping with red and gold and turquoise.

She smiled at the branches. "I always thought it could use a splash of color."

"I'm hoping more for a riot of color. With the water and the air and the different ways things are layered, I don't really know how it's going to look."

"A surprise."

"A surprise," he repeated.

He gently pushed her wrist toward the tree and guided her fingers to trace the folds of metal. He placed his hand over hers and walked her around the tree, guiding her over the roots. He stopped right before they made a full circle and she looked up at him, but he wasn't looking at her. She followed his gaze to back to the tree, where the fabric parted to reveal a patch of bark that looked like it had been carved. A heart, with the letters "WS loves LA."

She let out a sob, or a laugh, or a sobby laugh. She had no idea what kind of sound she was making. It was the cheesiest thing she had ever seen, and the most beautiful. It was ridiculous, and it was perfect.

At least, she thought it was perfect.

"This means me, right? You and me?" she asked.

He raised his eyebrows and opened his mouth, but he seemed to change his mind. He just smiled at her and nodded.

"You love me?"

He nodded again.

It was her turn for an eyebrow raise.

"You're gonna make me say it?" he asked.

"I'm not going to make you . . ." She shrugged, and started to turn away, but he caught her face in his hands.

"Lindsey Alford, I love you. I'm sorry for the crap I said when I was pissed at my father. I didn't mean it."

"Yes, you did."

He looked at her for a second, and she stood there, waiting.

"Yeah, I did. But only a little."

"How, exactly, is this romantic?"

"I don't think you're naïve. That's not what I meant. I meant that I am a crabby bastard, and you force me to see the bright side of things."

"And you don't always like it?"

"I can't promise I always will. I've been a crabby bastard for a long time. I'm used to it."

She put her hand on his wrist and held on. "Good thing I like you, even when you're crabby."

He rested his forehead on hers. "I need you, Lindsey."

She closed her eyes and breathed him in. Her Walker. "Okay," she said. *I need you, too,* she wanted to add, but then Walker had her around the waist and had his mouth on hers and she held on for dear life as he kissed and spun and kissed and nearly dropped her when he tripped over Booger.

"Okay," she said, once her feet were on the ground. "Okay, I got it." She kissed him again, just to make sure. "I love you, too."

"Let's never fight again."

She snorted at him. "How about, let's always have great make-up sex." She was getting more realistic, but she could still look on the bright side.

"Perfect," he said softly, and he kissed her.

That was it. There it was. Booger sniffed and walked around in a circle and then in another circle and lay down with his head on the roots of the tree.

"It is a truth universally acknowledged that a single woman in
possession of a ramshackle house must be in want of a handyman."

Just because English professor Grace Williams is a woman whose
"new" house is crumbling around her doesn't mean she needs an
arrogant, condescending man's help, even if he does look gorgeous
in faded jeans and a tool belt. What she needs is a working
bathroom, not a ridiculous crush.

Jake Burdette has no use for the university types who stumble
around Willow Springs, with their noses in the air whenever they're
not in a book. He may not be a scholar, but he's proud of the hard,
honest work he does—even if he would appreciate a little more of it.
He doesn't need Grace's pity, even if he does wish she wasn't so
adorably sexy.

They're all wrong for each other. But Grace's troublesome house
seems to feel differently . . .

Turn up the heat...

SNOWED IN

A Southern Comfort Novella

Sarah Title

There's nothing like a hot kiss on a cold day...

Librarian Maureen O'Connell might have predicted she'd find
herself crying into the ice cream case at the supermarket after a bad
breakup—but she definitely never imagined that a guy hot enough
to melt the Rocky Road would flirt with her right there in the freezer
aisle. Only Gavin Fraser isn't a fantasy, he's a mouth-watering new
flavor...

When a freak snowstorm strands Maureen at Gavin's after just one
date, it's a perfect excuse for something a lot steamier than hot
chocolate in front of the fire. It's definitely lust. Can it also be love?

Emily Bacon

Sarah Title has worked as a barista, a secretary, a furniture painter, and once managed a team of giant walking beans. She currently leads a much more normal life as a librarian in West Virginia. *Kentucky Home* is her first novel. You can visit her at www.sarahtitle.com.